Crannóg 60 spring 2024

GW00500781

ISSN 1649-4865
ISBN 978-1-907017-70-4

Cover image: *Evergreen Ivy* by Linda Keohane
Cover image sourced by Sandra Bunting
Cover design by Wordsonthestreet
Published by Wordsonthestreet for Crannóg magazine @CrannogM
www.wordsonthestreet.com @wordsstreet

Comhairle Cathrach na Gaillimhe
Galway City Council

CONTENTS

Submissions for Crannóg 61 open May 1st until May 31st
Publication date is September 27th 2024

Crannóg is published bi-annually in spring and autumn.

Submission Times:
Month of November for spring issue.
Month of May for autumn issue.

We will <u>not read</u> submissions sent outside these times.

POETRY:
Send no more than three poems. Each poem should be under 50 lines.
PROSE:
Send one story. Stories should be under 2,000 words.

We do not accept postal submissions.
When emailing your submission we require three things:
  1. *The text of your submission as a Word attachment.*
  2. *A brief bio in the third person.*
  3. *A postal address for contributor's copy in the event of*
     publication.

For full submission details, to learn more about Crannóg magazine,
to purchase copies of the current issue or take out a subscription,
log on to our website:

www.crannogmagazine.com

The Crannóg Bursary

Crannóg has been publishing poetry and short fiction since 2002. Over the intervening years it has grown and developed as a literary magazine that is now read all over the English-speaking world.

New features have been added such as the author interview which gives an insight into the writing lives of a variety of diverse authors. The website includes further material such as essays, memoir pieces, and articles on writing, all by writers and about writing.

To coincide with the 60th issue we are announcing the award of a Crannóg Bursary to one contributor to each issue of the magazine.

When each contributor to Crannóg is accepted for inclusion they are invited to make a short, simple application for the bursary.

The bursary amounts to €1500 per issue. We are delighted to celebrate the 60th issue with this further milestone in Crannóg's growth and development.

We are grateful to writer Marian Kilcoyne for her sponsorship of the Crannóg Bursary.

Editors

Tell Me Things

Beth O'Halloran

'I'VE BROUGHT YOU SOME ... UM ... reasons-to-stay-alive things,' she begins, trying not to let her eyes glom onto his bandages. She is sitting on a vinyl chair, which she slides too quickly and too close to the metal frame of his bed so her fingers get pinched. Wagging them, she pulls a big plastic box out of a bag.

'First up ... some beauties from my son's rock collection.' The box rattles as she levels it in the space between his knees and the edge of the bed. The box is divided into many small sections giving each rock a frame. 'These are the ones he says get top-shelf treatment.'

The tubes slow and stiffen his arm's movements like a puppet's. He's turning a sliver of geode in his fingers, placing it in front of one eye, while closing the other. 'Look at that,' he says, 'hard to believe it's of this earth ...' She nods, relieved that there is something for them to look at that is not his sliced-up arms.

How many times has she picked up a pebble and thought, this tiny thing will outlast us all, and the idea had shrunk her worries.

His hospital gown is covered in a broken-diamond pattern that looks like shiny things in cartoons. He's tapping a piece of what she thought was pink granite with his sallow fingers. He knows the proper name for it, but as soon as he says it, she forgets. Now, he's lifting a long, thin crystal – it looks like an icicle.

They've barely spoken since they shared joints on the college fire-escape, years ago. She doesn't know him well enough for this visit. Doesn't even know how far away to sit.

Before he has time to study each rock, she says, 'I have more ...' and her hand dives back into the bag.

Outside his window, there is a view of a giant beech tree with Halloween decorations dangling from the lowest branches. In the wind, the leaves flip from pale green to plum. Which only makes her think of his bruises. She wishes she could open the window. Her mouth is blotting-paper dry. She sees his plastic cup beside his bed, with a bent straw in it. 'Are you thirsty? she asks.

He's saying thank you ... but I'm ok. Thank you for coming all this way. And sorry. Sorry for scaring everyone. And for not being able to give you even a drop of tea after the long drive.

She hands him a small Tupperware container which contains a sprig of a pine-needled branch. There's a note written in a child's hand *Christmas 2016. Branch from Christmas Tree. Crystal growing.* 'I'm really not sure what this was – maybe there were salt crystals growing in here, but the thing I wanted to share with you ... open it ... can you smell it?' she asks, as he leans his face down. She listens to the sound of his breath and clings to it like a favourite song coming from a passing car. He closes his eyes. 'A pocket of Christmas,' he says.

'Five years on and still ...'

Maybe it was pine smell, but he's perked up a bit. Asks if she can help him shift the pillows so he can sit up more. 'When they brought me here – in the ambulance – they didn't put the siren on. I don't know why because they were going fast. I could tell because as I was lying there, I could see the blur from the skylight. Did you know they have skylights in ambulances?' No, she did not. 'Everything was quiet once the medic lady stopped asking me those next-of-kin questions. I was lying back and saw only sky and trees – you know the kind that look like they're reaching for each other. And the ambulance's blue light on the branches as we passed under them. I thought about whoever it was who decided to add those windows. And the kindness of that ... it helped. You know.'

She nods, her throat going solid. She is busy in her bag again. When he sees a woebegone plant, he laughs a laugh that becomes a cough – the kind of cough when a smoker hasn't got a cigarette. 'A succulent. My favourite,' he says. He turns the plant – which is not much bigger than his hand – a full 360 degrees, grins and says, 'Are you giving me this so I have to stick around and take care of it?'

Which reminds her that she was told – after having brought a potted flower to a funeral – to never bring potted flowers to a funeral – just cut flowers so the mourner won't be stuck with something that reminds them day in and day out of how long it has been since their loved one died and how this plant can go on living when they didn't.

'Maybe? Stick around or the succulent gets it,' she says and he coughs again.

'Look,' she says, 'the thing ... the real thing I wanted to say to you is ...' He's looking at her in a *Please don't* kind of way. She glances again at the beech tree. There is a crepe-paper skeleton with accordion limbs spinning. She's wondering why in God's name anyone put a decoration like that outside a rehab hospital. She continues, '... remember those paintings you did in college – the white ones.'

'Sorry? Paintings? I haven't ... in years.'

'I know, I know. It's not about them or doing things and all that. It's that I wanted to tell you ... it was the way you could always see more than the rest of us could. All the colours in the white. I never forgot those paintings.'

'Were they the ones we had to do? The crockery and crap?'

'Yes, some exercise. But the point is ... the point of this is ...'

'I know what you're trying to say. And thanks.'

'Can I just finish?' her voice hot. His eyebrows lift and she shifts her weight in the chair. 'I wanted you to know that every single time I look at the sky or I'm on a plane looking down at the whole carpet of white, I think about you and I see the yellows and purples and all that in the clouds. And it makes me think about how much ... how much I never said ... and ... thank you.'

'Now you look,' he says, but doesn't say anything else after.

There must be some roadworks nearby as men in hard hats pass the window.

'Are you in pain?' she asks, her chin pointing at the wounds.

'Not right now. They're giving me the good stuff. I swear it's worth it.'

'They're not worried about ...?'

'No, they know about all of that, of course. They just push the medication trolley out faster than I could reach for any of it. Warp speed. With all this' – he makes an arc with his fingers towards the IV and monitor – 'I'm as well behaved as a show dog.'

'Y'know there's a guy I'm going to set you up with once you feel up to such things again.'

'Yeah? Tell me about him.'

'He's got a beard ...'

'Sounds perfect.'

She snorts. 'Honestly, you'd like him. I met him when we were both waiting for an interview. He kept moving his feet. He was shifting so much, I asked him if he was ok. And he said he was moving because he had a pebble in his shoe. And I asked him why he wasn't taking it out. And he said he'd put it there on purpose. He said he was really nervous about the interview and so he'd put the pebble in because he knew he'd end up thinking about his sore foot instead of how nervous he was. He said he'd tried it before and it had worked.'

'A beard and a strategy. Sign me up. 'He's rolling a grain of soil from the plant between his thumb and forefinger. 'Now, I get to ask you how you are doing. It's only been ... a decade? More?'

'Ah y'know. I'm ok. The kids – both kids – are great. You'd love them – I've cooked friends from scratch.' His breath makes a sound again which she wants to sew into her seams. 'But ... I nearly forgot the drawings,' she says, her hand back in the bag.

He opens the sketchbook – it's her son's – as if it's a manuscript. 'What am I looking at? Jungles?'

'They're his terrariums.'

'Jesus Christ. Look at all the mushrooms. The details.'

'I know, crazy good aren't they?'

'Fucking hell. I swear to you, these drawings ... how old did you say he was again ... fucking hell. These drawings make me believe in God. And all the mushrooms.'

'He does them from his head. Swear, he's not looking at anything.' She's looking out the window again in a series of too-frequent glances.

'Wish all the mushrooms I took made my head work like this,' he says. The room becomes briefly lit by a reflection from a large metal sheet which two workmen carry past the window. He closes the sketchbook, looks hard at her and adds, 'You've driven a long way to come here.'

'Yeah. I needed you to know.'

'Know what exactly? It's not just to show me your Mary Poppins bag. You're pissed off with me, aren't you? Or is this one of your do-good things? I remember all your "causes".' He rolls his eyes and reaches for his cup.

'Jesus. That's a little below the belt isn't it?'

'I get to play the no bullshit card for quite some time now, I reckon.'

She considers standing up. Her hands roll into fists.

'Well, yeah, I guess you do. And I guess I am pissed off. But it feels mean to say that to you.' A shift of the chair which is a cumbersome lump – her legs are stuck to the plastic surface. She reaches for her bag again, but doesn't have anything left to pull out. She can't tell him how barren her intimate life has become since the divorce.

He's making his lips into a thin line. 'It's ok. If it helps, 110% of people who know me are pissed off with me. And you know how much I like it when people say 110%.'

'Stop making me laugh. I'm busy being pissed off. I wanted to come here and remind you of the things – I have a whole list in my head – cinnamon toast, hand-knitted things. Rain on corrugated tin. Knowing people who can see colours in white. But I'm so angry with you for nearly taking yourself and those parts of all the rest of us – the parts that we only get to be with you. I need you to be here so I can be the me I am with you.'

'That's pretty selfish.'

'I know.'

The workmen pass with empty arms. They wear clothes with many pockets. Gloves and wires are sticking out and there are powdery white marks the size of fingerprints all over their legs and arms. These capable men with their work-heavy boots and ways to fix things.

'I better head. The traffic will get bad. Plus you look tired.'

'Yeah. I feel like death warmed up. Can I ask you a favour?'

'Course.'

'I know you don't smoke, but would you pretend you do and have a cigarette for me?'

'That'll make me feel like crap.'

'I know.'

She gathers her things. One of her feet has fallen asleep from how awkwardly she had to sit in the semi-circle chair. She stands up and stamps her numb foot. 'Look at that,' he says, 'I'm your pebble.'

As she passes his window, she lets her fast walk break into a run – partly from relief of being out and partly to punish him with the life coursing through her.

The Mansion

Patrick Deeley

You bury your body under cold hard pellets of oats.
You suck air through a straw pipe, musty air
that makes you swallow your cough.
Steadily the oats heat; an itch eats behind your eyelids.
You are hiding from Them. Waiting

as you once waited among paint cans, mousetraps
and brooms, in the cubbyhole
under the stairs, the creak of the treads
as your siblings trudged above your head, the 3-legged L
of the cobbler's last squatting

beside you in the dark, shivery anticipations
and specks of dust taking your eye
and breath. Waiting as you have always done, to be
chosen – for a team, a trouble,
for yourself alone. Waiting on the flutter of ecstasy

that might cause you to lose your grip,
cast off the correct and sensible.
Suddenly, Them, the thump-heels of their boots
kicking the saddle stones on which
the granary sits, their fingernails scraping

the side panels of pine. They pet the oats, lift fistfuls,
sniff. Brink of discovery – a terror,
a thrilling ache. 'Nah' – their voices tail away.
'Nobody.' You drag yourself up,
slip, scramble for the light. Inside your skull

a mansion floats, its rooms now dark and airless, now
criss-crossed with sunshine. You pass
through the altered afternoon,
your eyes fixed on a nook where a poem
playing – making the shape of a ghost moth darts awake.

My Mother as a Silver Birch

Elizabeth Barton

I am old as the Ice Age,
limbs cobwebbed with lichen,

moss at my feet, fallen leaves thorned
with frost, a memory of wolves

in my roots. The knots in my trunk
are the glowering eyes of eagle owls.

My crimson cones are tongues
whispering in an ancient language,

my windblown seeds are immortal.
Beneath my peeling bark, beetles carve

myths on my belly. My crown is bowed,
as though I bear all the sorrow of the world

on frail shoulders. I long to see the stars
but my view has shrunk to a silver pool

reflecting ghostly branches. I am pared
to essentials, the wind plucking my strings

of fear and wonder like a Welsh harp.
I am a perch for a woodlark,

I am the ladder you must climb to write
on the skin of the moon.

If You're Quiet Enough

Ana Reisens

You can hear the pines reach out
to embrace you –

the whittled hollows
of their skin, the lattice
of their branches, the yearning
to be rooted and reaching
all at once.

All of this is here to greet you.

The chickadee watches
from a slender branch, feathers
brushed with wind, as the clouds
break and the rain carries itself
into the distance.

We were never meant
to break away from this:

the branches, the rain,
the breathless rustle of the wind.
The hills glisten with everything
I was meant to tell you but could
not say, everything that sounds
like feathers and rain but
really just means thank you,
I am here with you,
I love you.

The Fall

David Butler

THAT YEAR THE WEATHER WAS TOPSY-TURVY. Weeks of drought, then it said on the news that June had been the wettest since records began. Nana said the garden didn't know whether it was coming or going. And none of it would have mattered, if only Oisín hadn't brought Darren Roche back with him.

Cian trailed a good half field behind them. Too far to make out what Roche was muttering into Oisín's ear, his elbow on Oisín's shoulder like they were lifelong buddies. Too far for them to be able to turn on him again, to chase him away. 'Fuck off home, *child*,' Roche had taunted, making a feint toward him with one fist pulled back. Then his brother repeated it. 'Yeah, fuck off home, Cian.' Oisín, who never used bad language. That's why it pushed such a hard lump into his throat, far more painful than the bruise from that morning.

But he had to keep going, trailing after them. The days were huge and empty and endless, like the ache inside his stomach. It was yawning and empty, as if he was starving. But he wasn't even hungry. He slowed, pushed up the sleeve of his T-shirt, twisted the skin till he could see the bruise. Would it be like the bad of an apple underneath, crumbly and sickly sweet? He put his mouth around it and sucked. It tasted of salt. It wasn't as if the bruise hurt much anymore. What hurt so he could feel it inside him like an ache was that Oisín had taken this intruder up into the tree-house. Into their secret den. When he'd tried to follow them up, they'd turned his own ammo against him. They'd taken turns flinging used batteries down until a torch battery had struck him on the arm.

And it wasn't as if he was a 'child', either. He'd be twelve come September.

He'd be starting secondary school. Okay, Oisín was fourteen now. Last year his voice had broken. He'd shot up, got lanky. Gawky, Nana called it. He wore longers, even in summer. Then he'd insisted on going to the Gaeltacht in Dingle. Oisín, who hated Irish. That's why June had been such a long, miserable month. It wasn't just the rain. Down in Nana's, there was nothing to do when Oisín wasn't there. The farm was just a stupid farm.

When he was seven and Oisín nine or ten, their mam had run off to Galway. After that their da packed them off every summer holidays out to Nana's. The old farm was about twenty minutes' drive outside Tralee. There was no way you could walk it back home. It wasn't a working farm, not since their grandfather had died, and that was before Cian was born. A neighbour called McGowan paid rent so his cattle could graze the overgrown fields and he could cut silage in giant black plastic rolls. But their da told Nana he was only paying her pin money.

Why do we always have to go *there*? Oisín moaned, every single June. It's *boring*. Because the pair of you couldn't be trusted, mooching around town all day with no-one to keep an eye on you. Besides, it's no harm to keep in with the old dear for fear she might take a notion and give the place away. He'd said that with a wink, to make a joke out of it. But it didn't feel like a joke. Oisín didn't smile back. He breathed loudly through his nose. So how come he couldn't bring a friend? Ask Nana, I'm not stopping you. Oisín frowned at this, puzzled. He'd expected objections. But half the class were going to the Gaeltacht that year. It wasn't fair he couldn't go. Then their da gave in on that one, too.

That was why, all through June, Cian couldn't wait for July. But then yesterday Oisín showed up off the bus with Darren Roche, with his sly eyes and whispery sniggers. They both had these stupid haircuts. Shaved at the back and sides right up above the ears but long on top and flopping down over their foreheads. Nana, who was from Dublin originally, said they looked like a right pair of chuckeroes. They smirked at each other as if she was being funny. It would've been different if Cian could've had a friend out to stay. But his best friend in school was Sorcha Ní Riada. You couldn't ask a girl to stay over, though the idea gave him a woozy feeling. Their da would make a big joke out of it. And Oisin would've called him a sissy.

He was trailing behind them now because he was sure Oisín was going to show this stranger all their secret places. To betray them, one after another. To laugh at them. Over the years, he and Oisín had transformed the farm into a country. The kingdom of Asgard it was called, after the boat Oisín said had run the guns for the Easter Rising. Except, their Asgard was set two hundred years ago. Its colours were black and red. When the buddleia filled up with butterflies, the red admirals were the ships of the Asgard fleet. The peacocks and tortoiseshells were from Nagria, which was constantly making war on Asgard.

Already, the pair ahead had kicked apart the miniature bridge he and Oisín had built over the ditch which was really the mighty river Volta. Last summer they'd fought a pitched battle there, the toy soldiers lined up on either bank, red and black for Asgard, purple and yellow for the Nagrians. They'd named each Asgard regiment and made flags for them. Oisín said that Cian's regiment couldn't be hussars because they didn't have horses, but they could be dragoons because dragoons travelled on horseback but fought on foot. They'd thrown batteries for artillery and used darts for musket fire and the battle lasted a whole week.

But now the bridge was kicked asunder, and the two were heading for the abandoned house, which was the ruined city of Inver. Three years ago, they'd found a folded-up Ordnance Survey map of the farm up in Nana's attic, yellowing with black lines showing the lane and the fields and outhouses. It opened up to the size of a table-cloth. Over the months they'd added colours, place-names, crossed swords where battles had taken place. They filled up four copybooks they called the Asgard Chronicles. It was an entire history of Asgard, like you'd find in a museum or somewhere. With a plunging sense of dread, Cian remembered they kept map and copybooks in the war chest up in the tree-house.

He ran at a lope till his side hurt and his breath came raw and shallow. Once, he stopped to use his inhaler and to hold together the stitch in his side. Through wet eyes the great oak wobbled into view. He paused again, one hand against the trunk, doubled over to get his breath back. Then he scrambled up the rough and ready rungs they'd hammered into the tree and pushed his torso up through the trapdoor. The war chest, an old trunk they'd also found in Nana's attic, stood where it always stood. He could even make out the chain with the combination padlock. He levered himself up onto the platform, crawled to the chest, fiddled with the lock with mutinous fingers. On the third attempt it opened.

There was something thrown in on top that shouldn't be in there, no way. His stomach turned a somersault. Though he'd never seen one, he knew what it was. A porn mag. Grown-up girls with big breasts. Not like the girls in his class. Not like Sorcha Ní Riada. But under their cardigans the women teachers had them. Miss O'Dowd who taught fourth class was even called the Top Heavy Fraction.

But the picture the porn mag was open on was nothing like that. It showed this woman crawling across the floor. She was looking back over her shoulder straight at the camera. And her rear end was up. And her bits were on show. And they were swollen and gaping and mud-coloured. He flung it from him, scrambled crablike backwards, all but fell through the trapdoor.

His hand groped blind for the rope underneath. His foot slipped from a rung. He swung out sideways. A branch barked his shin. Another slammed his jaw shut. Then he was mid-air. Had shock and shame made his fingers lose their grip, or the hot tears which were blurring the world, or could it be that he'd wanted to fall, indignation making him deliberately careless?

Even as hip and spine and the back of his head slammed into the ground and he felt the thud rock up through his frame, he knew there would be just one moment of calm before his body was overwhelmed with the pain of it.

The Minotaur

Luke Power

I once lost myself in my head on the regular
for want of a firmer foundation to plant my mind.
Now and again I cut the clew by which Theseus made it out;
I came to know the Minotaur better than I should,
better than some, though all learn his name given time.
You get tired of this; submitting to a legendary monster
grew old, and I drew nearer growing horns myself
and taking his place, giving him my PPS number,
a map and the keys to a fast car.
He'd have made better use of them than me, he'd have got further.

But the time came; though I didn't slay the beast I left his land
and picked up the threads from where they lay, a little greyer
than I was but a little cuter also, a little bit more
in the way of wiles and I had a future, God damn it.
I found God, and lost Him, sometimes I put Him in the maze
with the Minotaur, which had its advantages,
next I was in there myself.
I don't spend much time there anymore,
though the Minotaur remembers my name
and has the kettle on for me should I ever visit.

I crossed the water to a neighbouring island,
having crafted wings which could withstand the heat,
and I live there now. It has a population of two,
though if it didn't, I may be tempted by times
to fly back, I can still see the walls from where I lay.

Perhaps God might join us here someday;
perhaps we could put Him up in the spare room
though I suspect He has too much work to do in the maze
for taking up residence on the coast.
We'll wait; here or there, we'll meet Him again,
standing in the last cul-de-sac,
the ancient bull casting sand upwards
and lowering his quivering head for the charge.

Spun

Alicia Byrne Keane

I'm not sure I have the space to limn again
the blue threads of the walk I was just on,
I might run into a shopping list
or a page of journalled fears.
I felt a tug in my stomach
by the streams – so much black water flashing
between slabs of stone. Low lying banks bright
with moss, the land cut into platforms
so you can see where the water has lain and worn.
I suppose I am examining the minutes
since I met you. I suppose I'm not letting a single
one out of my sight. It has given me a lot
to write about, and made me a boring dinner party guest.
Here in the line of gorse by the road: hundreds
of spiderwebs hung with rain.
It has been drizzling – breath-like enough, maybe,
to let nothing here fall between thorns.

I wrote about the same boy, a spell upon him, closed
from us behind a screen of thorns, our lives desolate with waiting,
you said you imagine what it was like to be that boy
unable to move as the briars grew towards you,
feeling the prick of them, like daggers on your skin.

I said at least you were loved, all three of us loved you,
you said you knew, but it was missing the point;
maybe some days you wanted to carry on watching TV and not pack
an overnight bag,
maybe some days you wanted to go to a friend's house after school
and not ours or hers
and maybe some days you wanted to say what you really meant
without
worrying about taking sides
but it didn't matter, it was all in the past now,
I said I was sorry; we thought we were doing the right thing.

Here we are thirty years on still trying to make it alright.

February Past

Rachel Coventry

Her house was three slats of a pallet
balanced between silt and thicket.
She waited like a sleeping princess
for some latchiko to come along.

He still had a war in his eyes.
She, hypnotised by those pretty explosions.
He said he'd seen active service in Angola.
What that meant was inchoate;

what it meant was something rotted.
The war burst out of him at decreasing intervals
She had no walls to hide behind
but she planted crocuses in the loam of it.

Every year they detonated like a joke.
How they laughed and laughed
till their tears flowed.

Ten of Swords

Laura Demers

WHEN I FIRST GOT HERE, EVERYONE LIKED ME. I was prettier last fall, before I let Tracy cut my hair, before I got the pentagram tattoo on my neck. I was also accepted because of Paula, who let me share her tarot card table. It was on the northeast corner of Jackson Square, where Milo sets up shop now. She would send me out to put up the table while she had her coffee, and I loved the morning light on the square, the way it lit first the horse carriages and then the statue, how it made the Mississippi glitter in the distance. How even the pigeons with their iridescent wings seemed magical, more like doves.

I was clear-headed last autumn, too, and my readings were good enough to create a stir. I developed my own special technique for reading palms. Everyone says I learned it from Paula, but that's not true. She just taught me how to size up customers, how to look for obvious signs, like wedding rings, or tan lines from missing wedding rings, or scars. To listen to the timbre of the customer's voice to tell if they were cynical or sad or hopeful. How to be a little ambiguous, so that you could be right either way.

'Doing tarot is easier, ' Paula told me. 'The cards speak for you. Anything the cards say can be true.'

She promised to make me an expert at reading tarot cards, and she did teach me a lot before she gave up on me.

But the truth is, I didn't always hustle the customers. I honestly knew things without being told. About everyone, not just people whose palms I read. I wish I had never let anyone know this, though. I'm sure that's when the tide really turned against me. It was right after Paula left, and everyone was blaming me for her leaving.

Milo is coming towards me now, crossing the square from St. Ann Street. He never comes out until sunset, which is getting later and later every night. His eyes are puffy, and his dreadlocks are tucked into the back of his green flannel shirt. I know him well enough to know he's just woken up from a two or three-hour nap, that he's smoked some pot to get himself going. He doesn't look at me as he passes, and I feel ice in the pit of my stomach, as if this were the first time he's blanked me.

He doesn't see me at all anymore. None of them really look at me now, but Milo hurts the most. I wonder who he'll end up with tonight. He went home with a tourist last month, back to her hotel on Dauphine. I lurked around in the street like a masochist. I hadn't been following them, but I came across them on Toulouse. The tourist was pulling him by the hand, staggering a little in her ladylike heels. They were coming from the direction of Bourbon Street. She was one of those girls with clean yellow-blonde hair who travel in a pack with other girls with clean yellow-blonde hair and sound like a flock of geese. I couldn't believe Milo would choose her. I almost preferred it when he was with Tracy. I knew he was just using Tracy to hurt me, anyway.

The day Tracy cut my hair, I accused her of liking him. She changed the subject.

'Your hair is so damaged,' she said.

She said I should stop dyeing the ends purple. We were sitting outside Paula's room on the tiny balcony, and I was watching the wet purple locks drop around my chair. That was my last good day, with the sun on my legs and Tracy taking my head between her hands and telling me to hold still. She would stop occasionally to take a puff from her vape pen, and I remember staring out at the river and telling her I had thought we were friends. That she needed to stop flirting with Milo in front of me.

When Paula left and I had nowhere to go, I asked Tracy if I could stay in the room she rented, but she wouldn't even answer me. I knew where she kept her key, so I would sneak in and sleep when she was out on the square. But I still had to spend the nights on the street. I'd sit on the sidewalk with the Untouchables, Roy and Sid and Alice, while they called out plaintively to passing tourists. When they had collected enough money, they'd go and buy beer. Alice was always so high that she'd just stay behind, and I'd stay with her, trying not to look at her dirty, cut-up feet. She'd shift her feet and tug on the frayed hem of her jean shorts and say nothing.

Her eyes are always glassy, the pupils so dilated that the irises look almost black. I remember the shock when I first realised her eyes are actually bottle green. We had been sitting up all night, leaning against the wall on the corner of Chartres and Dumaine. I don't know where the two other Untouchables had gone. Alice's hands were twitching, and she began to scratch at her arms and legs.

As the sun rose, she turned to me and I saw how her eyes might normally look. It really scared me. I remember getting up and walking quickly away. I walked all around the perimeter of the French Quarter, ending up on Esplanade, where I passed the man who hands out fliers for the swamp tour.

When I came back, she was gone. There was just an empty can and some loose change left behind. I never knew where Alice went in the daytime. Wherever it was, I didn't want to think about it. I could pretty much guess.

She let me read her palm once. Or rather, she was drifting off, and I picked up her hand and looked at it without permission. She had a short life line, which didn't surprise me.

Another time, I held my hand out to her.

'Read my palm, Alice. I'll explain how to do it.'

I was desperate for some connection, some acknowledgment that I existed. She only picked at her nails and made a weird grimace.

A man moved into Paula's place not long after she left. I look up now from my corner of the square and see him on the tiny balcony. He's wearing silver shorts and drinking out of a wine glass. He's always brandishing his cocktail and calling out to people in the street. During Mardi Gras, he had a crush of four or five people on the tiny balcony. I kept watching in the crazy hope that Paula would appear up there.

Half the reason I won't leave Jackson Square is Paula, in case she comes back. I know they all think I'm lingering for Milo, but it's also for Paula. I really hurt her, and I want to apologise. I did take the money, that part is true, but I had every intention of putting it back the following day or the day after, as soon as I made the money back. If she had waited a couple of days to check the drawer, we would still be friends. She would still be in New Orleans, Milo would still be my boyfriend, and I wouldn't be hanging out with the zombie Untouchables.

I often forget what I took the money for. It wasn't much. Less than a hundred dollars. It's so hard to keep it in my mind, what the money was for. It slides out of my brain as soon as I get hold of it.

Oh, yes. For the tattoo. I took the money to get the tattoo. I touch my neck. It still feels infected. It oozes a little, even now. Milo has a pentagram on his neck, and I wanted one, too, to surprise him.

But everything got ruined. I have a blank in my mind around the tattoo. The last thing I remember is going into the dark doorway of the tattoo parlour.

A woman comes towards me now, my first customer in a long time. I sit up against the wrought-iron railing. Before she has even reached me, I know a lot about her. I know that she has breast cancer, and that she just found out. That her mother died of it around the same age she is now, which is maybe mid-forties. I know that she has a jewellery box where she keeps something no one knows about. I can't see what this thing is, but I know she can't decide what to do with whatever it is, because it's stolen.

A girl, maybe twelve or thirteen, scampers up and grabs the woman's hand just as she reaches me and pulls her away.

It's night now, the last of the sunset dissolving as the street lamps and store lights come on. I see Tracy coming towards me, ignoring Milo the same way he ignores me. She walks past him and sets up her table almost right in front of me. I can see the loose threads trailing from the hem of her tie-dye skirt, and her long pianist fingers laying out the decks of cards. I sit quietly while a tourist who's had too much to drink comes up to Tracy to get her cards read. Everything Tracy tells her is wrong. I hate Tracy for talking me into letting her cut my hair, for putting her table right in front of me, for making more money than I ever did, even though she doesn't have any sort of gift at all.

I get up and walk to Rouses Market and wander up and down the aisles, the lights fritzing and blinking, and then walk to where I got the tattoo. I touch my neck reflexively as I pass and feel a shiver of regret.

He's gone now, the man who gave me the tattoo. The store was permanently shut not long after I went in. A small strip of yellow barricade tape is still stuck to one side of the door.

Just then I see Alice, coming out of a side door. She stumbles a little on the street and puts her hand out to steady herself. I hesitate and then catch up with her. We go to sit outside a souvenir shop and wait for Roy and Sid to get back from wherever they've been. They eventually arrive with two cans of Miller Lite and a roast beef Subway sandwich and sit down next to us, sharing some of the sandwich with Alice. I spot Milo on a break and get up quickly to hide in the shadow of the alley, so he can't see me with the Untouchables.

When I sit back down, Alice turns my way and smiles, as if she knows why I hid and forgives me. She's in an opioid haze, but I feel grateful anyway, because Alice is the only one who will look in my direction. When Sid and Roy get up to wander away again, she stays with me.

After a while, I see the mother, the one with breast cancer, walking with her husband and kids. I watch them until they disappear down Chartres into the throng of tourists, and what the woman has stolen comes to me in a flash. It's a gold and diamond butterfly pin. The story of the pin is probably why she gravitated towards me. I want to tell her to just give it back, to wherever it came from, before it's too late.

But I'm guessing it's already too late for her, too.

Goldilocks

Patrick Devaney

For Clare

It was our pleasantest retreat:
You, almost three, ahead of us
On a visit to the forest park;
New leaves veiling beech and birch;
Thrush, chaffinch, linnet choiring joy
And you beside the lake, throwing crusts
To mallards in the lily-dappled bay ...

Then, the sunlit world left outside,
We are walking down pine-needled paths,
Entering the land of Goldilocks.
We may have paused to watch a squirrel
Or rested on a log while you explored
But when we look again, you're gone!
At first we call to you:
No answer, just the feral silence
Of the dark, indifferent conifers ...

Distraught we range about,
Moments lengthening to a lifetime,
Until we see you strolling down an aisle,
A spruce cone held in each raised hand.
I gaze as, lost in an inner world,
You move, indifferent to our presence.
Then when you come nearer
Sunlight falling through the canopy
Turns your hair bright gold...

Happy, I take your photo,
Never thinking that, grown up, you will stray
Deeper into a sunless forest
And maybe never hear my calls.

Blackbird

Stephen Shields

He was proud of his feathers,
black, neat with a dickie bow.
His beak darted in the hedge
the day he organised a concert;
no-one came, not even the thrush,
who at first had feigned interest.

Blackbird sang a lone tune,

'Sometimes there are things,
you just have to do. Why I do
not know. Try my therapist.
If you're on good terms, ask God;
me, I pour out music.
It's something I find imperative.'

Harvest

Anne Donnellan

I wake to fog-stuffed orchard
apple trees a ribcage
their skeleton branches jig with an easy breeze
sunlight veins breach cloud
show windfalls strewn on crimson leaves

From my rooftop
a sudden rattle
blackbird wrestles with a fallen apple
peck stab and gorge
till the gored remains
drop on the driveway gravel

I think of my father
his saving care for the crop
in the cool back cabin
on stilted timber crates
he stacked the lot
shielded from ravage of wind or bird
for our winter eating.

I'm not storing anything
let wind have its way
sweeten the day for hungry beaks
give song a chance

Falling

Attracta Fahy

After L-Young Lee

Under my bedroom skylight
I rest in night's slow pulse,
heavy eyes follow patterns,
a glass table of stars,
Bear, Plough, Pleiades.

From my garden
a thud
the last of the apples
falling

a rustle of leaves
they plummet through air
drop one
by one,
sometimes in two's,
three's

bump off the compost bin
rattling down before
a final thump
onto the pebbles beneath.

All night, one after another
they plunge,
half-sleeping I slip into dream.

As a child I didn't know life
would be like this –
collecting apples
after school,
how tough to pull stems
from a bough
yet, in the full blush of their own slow
ripening
they snap from their branch
and let go

They Know Us Here

Katherine Noone

Years of renting offered flexibility with work.
From Tenafly to Astoria to Manhattan
spaces got smaller yet more expensive.

Ten years in a large studio by the East river,
Gracie Mansion near by
lent round the clock security.

Our apartment had everything
kitchen to futon.
A wide window suffused in sunshine
even on Nine Eleven.

Here colleagues dropped in
bringing laments and laughter.
Little Olivia from across the hall
came here, on her first walk.

Finally, our own little place
in Galway, amidst family
and new found friends.
Near soothing sea and city scents.

Lucille

Beatte Sigriddaughter

THERE WAS A TIME WHEN I HAD FOUR beautiful daughters and no importance. I loved Mark, and I was powerless. He was busy, successful, charming, and popular. When he came home from his days at the office, the girls, egged on by me, would compete at winding themselves around his legs until everybody collapsed together on the sofa for a love festival. Except me. I was the bread and butter, the everyday, the all-day-long. He was the luxury. Oh, they liked me of course, and they depended on me. I was, after all, the provider of mundane needs. They also didn't like me. Even then. I was the one who said no too often for their taste, the one who took them to the dentist and made them put on clean underwear even though that took an extra effort in the excitement of starting a new day. They didn't like that at all.

Mark was a magical father. Bell, Liz, Mia, and Jas would continue to find chocolate Easter eggs in obscure places around the house until way into July. He got all the credit of course. And he deserved most of it. He was always a lot of fun. Then again, working as a corporate attorney all day and then entertaining four boisterously happy daughters at night took its toll. He had mastered the lesson that you should not ever take out your work frustration on your children. He may have missed the lesson that recommended you do the same for your stay-at-home wife. So, when things came to a boiling point, he'd snap at me from time to time. I could even understand that.

One of the hardest things for me was to not snap back at him. Raising four daughters had its own set of frustrations. We had agreed that I would stay at home until Jas, the youngest, was in school. I had some inkling that it would be hard to be a homemaker and mom after my own brief flirtation with a career, and I was prepared to make concessions. But I wasn't prepared to become completely insignificant.

Mark and I had met in law school. We were sparkling companions, both of us ambitious, attractive, bright, friendly – the perfect couple, proving that you could have it all. As homemaker mom, I missed that. Suddenly my brains felt as though they were melting, fading, shrinking. I remembered how exuberant I had once been studying for my bar exam even while my next-door neighbour's wind chimes kept chiming in the irritating wind. Oh, I was lovely then. And excited. And exciting. Now I was a stressed mom, getting just a wee bit tired of *Make Way for Ducklings* and 'Row, Row, Row Your Boat' and sewing Halloween costumes.

Instead of taking it out on Mark, I fell in love. Alex was in a vaguely similar situation. He was a freelance writer just beginning to get published in glossy magazines, though his income was sporadic. His wife provided the steady job as human resources manager in a burgeoning telecommunications company. It was only natural that he stayed at home with their two kids, Matt and Gabe. He dispensed baby aspirins, wiped noses, did laundry, cooked hot dogs. Like me, he was often judged inadequate and irritating, and above all unimportant.

We knew each other in passing from the school parking lot, from picking up kids from co-ed soccer games, from parent/teacher meetings, volunteer sessions, and so on, and it was while waiting in front of the principal's office for a dressing-down because my Bell and his Matt had participated in the organisation of a stupid prank that we first felt a spark between us. Shared mortification grew into shared laughter and then into hunger. Here was an attractive member of the opposite gender that didn't see me merely as a resource, a dependable convenience. When he looked at me, there was wonder in his eyes.

At first, we kept our affair apologetically secret – we were, after all, both basically decent and loyal human beings who were not out to rock any boats or hurt our families. However, we soon found out that we were both starved for affection, for approval, for admiration, and we found that we could feed each other's hunger. And so we did. He noticed the curve of my earlobes, the sunrays in my soul, the circus of longing in my hands. Eventually we decided we really liked the feast we provided for one another, and we deserved it. Jas and his younger son, Gabe, started school the same year. And we ran away together. All the way from Colorado to Arizona. I got a job in a law office immediately, and he had more and more success with his freelance writing.

We lived frugally and we were happy. We both sent home money for childcare.

Mark was devastated. People who had known us as a couple thought I was plain stupid. Such a nice guy. How could I? My daughters were even madder at me than in the old days when I had merely been a mildly burdensome presence thwarting some of their most extravagant schemes. Both Alex and I filed for divorce. Mark agreed. Alex's wife did not. Still, we lived together in beautiful Arizona, hiked in the marvels of the Grand Canyon, and lay in each other's arms until our insignificance went into remission.

It lasted a glorious year. Alex's wife ultimately prevailed, and he returned to her. He was reluctant to abandon our fairy tale, but he realised he was deep down a family man and had already once committed himself to his original family, and that was that. I wished him well. I can imagine the gossip surrounding me and Mark. 'And she didn't even stay with the other guy. It barely lasted a year. He'll never take her back. I wouldn't.' And Mark didn't. I knew he wouldn't, so I didn't even try.

Two years after I left, Mark married his secretary, and she was happy to be a mom to our daughters as they entered their teens one by one. He grudgingly let me spend time with our girls in their summer vacations. They gradually came to love me again and even came to understand what they had first experienced only as desertion. I hope they will have it easier. Our world being what it is, I am sceptical.

I am happy. I am alone. We all thrive on the nectar of attention, but we can exist without it. At times I listen to Kenny Rogers' 'Lucille' and similar songs on my iPod, songs that remind me I was born into a world where men above all respect and honour one another. A woman who looks for pleasure or importance for herself is out of order and often out of luck as well. All things considered, I have done well for myself. Sometimes I wonder how each of my daughters would tell this story.

I miss my illusions, but I have four beautiful daughters who are beginning to understand me, and I am important.

And Disappoint Turns To –

Mary Melvin Geoghegan

I'm not sure
why we were heading
for St. Joseph's Church, in Carrickmacross
against the rain and wind.
Perhaps, to light a candle.
The front door was locked
no give, around the back the same
another twist and we're inside.
I'd almost forgotten –
all those Harry Clarke stained glass windows
and St. Ceara's designed by Clarke himself.
Waiting – to be admired, devoured
like glistening jellies
as pristine and glorious
as on the day almost a century ago.
The artist had imagined the glass
seduced the pigment
inoculating our senses
against –

Imagine

Emily Cullen

if we took time to make tallow
to follow our ancestors who rendered
the fat of sheep for candles
on days there was no paraffin

who melted it down, let suet
simmer for two hours, then rolled
it round a twine of wick, snipping
the top about four inches, we might

dwell more on the here and now
if we made tapers to glow, glimmer
in winter months, dark and fallow
if we took time to make tallow.

Yard Work

Brian Gourley

I take the cast iron black shovel in one hand
and the green plastic rake in the other
and gather up the dead leaves,
the fallen twigs, the rain-rotted grass,
in short, everything once natural
and now browning, yellowing,
in differing states of decay.
I take the rake, pile the cast-offs
into the brown bin:
the shark-finned brambles
that I've hacked down to the base;
it's done every year
but then returns without fail.
I shovel up the upturned grass;
the reedy tough tussocks
lie decapitated. Next spring's flowers
will be planted next week
and the revolution
will proceed to its next stage;
it's what must be done.
The citizen's right and obligation
as a member of the republic of humanity
to overthrow and make anew,
first sword, then ploughshare,
the bare soil is open terrain;
today I have begun.

Caught in the Flow

Sandra Bunting

of the wild river,
the flow of conversation on Shop Street,
flow of music in the Crane bar,
a net of herring, a hooker out on the bay,
red sails flapping, silver water-sky thread,
golden light behind a wall of rain,
down there mullet bottom feeders,
a swan spills into Claddagh basin
in an up-and-down carnival ride,
one white gleaming feather lifts high
in the rough swirling wind.

Caught in the flow of the canal,
a mangled crow's tree
under which chestnuts roll,
the flow to catch bluebells in old woods,
a snail leaving tracks on your skin,
the madmen get under your skin,
buskers dance in all directions,
the city points west into a heart of fog.

Statuary

Saoirse McCann Callanan

WELL, I'VE ALWAYS LIKED THE WORD, he tells them.

Statuary. Your mouth and tongue take on all manner of shapes when you say it. Do it now, he says, and they oblige. They shrug, unimpressed.

The rest is difficult to explain. The truth eludes even him.

He yearns for the distant day when the words spark from him like misplaced electricity, a live wire cut open; when he takes up a pen and writes until the muscles of his wrist spasm. He imagines leatherbound tomes processed through an ancient printing press, distributed with whispered instructions. Him nailing pages to church doors. It will seem to passers-by that the silver nails are churned from his very hand, wrought into being by the fever of his need alone.

Those first moments of the day are holy. After bathing in the weak dawn light, he balances the plastic pot on the edge of the sink. In his mind he sees a steel-coloured butterfly emerge from its cocoon. He stirs the paint with the brush, hypnotised. The brush takes on its own life then, the soft-slick strokes beginning at his ankles, gliding from knee to thigh, circling his navel. He and the mirror are the same species. He leans into his reflection.

Caroline does not look at him when he comes down the stairs, his silver-painted brogues creaking. She looks instead into an empty cereal bowl, at white dregs of milk. He sits opposite her in silence, folds his hands on the table, and becomes utterly still. She takes her bowl to the sink and leaves the house, slamming the door behind her.

When she leaves his posture relaxes and he drinks her abandoned coffee. He prefers not to eat in the mornings; he considers it fasting on semi-religious grounds. When he removes the cup from his mouth the rim is printed silver, the surface of the coffee like an oil-slick. He tilts it back and forth, watching its iridescent progress.

In the day he shines. On the silver cardboard podium he stands a foot above the world, a sign written in divine paint propped at his feet: ARGENTO. He no longer bothers to bring the tin box with him; he considers it a form of tithing. He told himself from the start that he would not be corrupted by his newfound power. When a child stops in its tracks before him, Argento wants to shout, I too am mortal, my child. My beauty but skin-deep; my blood like yours.

Instead, with a practised flourish, he removes his silver hat and bows to the child, until it is jerked in the other direction by its parent.

Standing before Argento, a person lives a life exaggerated. They feel the urgent need to compensate for his inertia with movement of their own. In front of him they spring to action like wound-up toys. They press close to each other and kiss open-mouthed. They dance, spinning their partners on upraised hands, rolling them back into their chests. They contort their faces into caricatures, grotesque and beautiful. They collapse with laughter at his feet.

He is their mirror, and they shine in his light.

When he grants them movement, they cheer on his resurrection.

Children are his main disciples. They flock to his feet like doves.

At home his daughter Agnes writhes crying in his arms.

I don't blame her, he says later. Without the paint I look like a shelled lobster.

At least you don't look like a salmon, Caroline says.

He studies the remnants of silver on his fingernails. He does not tell her that only when he is painted does he feel God, stirring in him like a dormant beast.

He urges Caroline to join him on the podium. She says, Yes John, of course I would love to spend the day painted silver, standing on a piece of cardboard like a fool. What better things have I to do with my time? He asks that she please call him Argento, as he has asked many times before. She assures him that when the divorce papers arrive they will be addressed to Argento.

He begins to call her Patina.

On the first morning the paint had burned his skin. He found himself unable to achieve a smooth line with the brush. Everywhere he looked were brushstrokes that proved his tint unnatural, chinks in his armour. He had not opened the windows and the fumes made his head weak.

Caroline helped him into his wedding suit, which they had spent the night painting silver. He bent his elbows and the cheap paint cracked. He watched flecks of silver drift to the ground like chromatic snow. She raised his chin with her finger and kissed his lips.

When she withdrew her lips shimmered.

The courage inspired by Caroline was extinguished when he found himself alone and fluorescent in the sun. He paced, dazzling along the streets, head bowed, breaking into a near run when a youth called him a silver wanker.

He had taken Caroline location-scouting the day before. Their search was unfruitful and, exhausted, she had sat on an old bench with her hand resting on her swollen stomach. She said that he was impossible. Her forehead glistened and the cloud-filtered sunlight turned her sweat to molten silver. Triumphant, he said, this is it. This is where I will begin.

At first he had found it difficult to sit still, his limbs itching with restrained movement. When a stranger dropped a coin into the tin box the rattle would startle him and he would fumble his movements. Once, his hat dropped to the ground and the wind carried it from him. He drew in a shallow breath. Before he could stand, a boy ran from the crowd with the hat in his hands and, half-kneeling, proffered it to the silver man.

After a moment of awed silence, Argento's limbs had become unstuck. With his first movement of perfect mechanical rhythm, he leaned his head forward and allowed the boy to place it on his head. There had been a smattering of applause before the small crowd dispersed.

Argento says, Maybe I should just leave the paint on overnight instead of taking it off. It's such a hassle, taking it off and putting it on again. Patina raises her eyebrows.

He sits at the dinner table silver, and when he picks up the cutlery it appears to have sprouted from his skin. Agnes laughs. Argento, in smooth robotic motions, begins to creep towards her, holding the knife and fork aloft. Agnes screams with delight.

When he undresses, Patina asks why on earth he paints himself in places nobody but her will see. That can't be healthy, she says, pointing down.

The following morning she stands over him. Her body is stained seal-pup grey.

This has to stop, she says. Paint yourself all you want but keep it out of my house.

She points to his wedding band. Isn't that silver enough for you?

Argento twists the ring on his finger, camouflaged by the paint.

Why do you do it, John? she said, sitting next to him. Can't you see yourself?

I do it for the money.

What money?

Argento reaches behind his ear and produces a silver coin. He presents it to her on an open palm. It is the latest addition to his performance.

I'm going out, she says, and disappears.

Argento does not waste time. He props Agnes on the changing table and she remains still while he paints her with delicate strokes. She only blinks, her eyelashes limned silver.

He lifts Agnes above his head and marvels at his creation.

Before they leave Argento writes '& CHILD' on his sign.

Cars slow on the road as they pass. People rush to windows to watch the slow pilgrimage. Behind them gathers a parade of onlookers, following from a reverent distance.

They cannot resist, he whispers to Agnes. Like magpies they are, and us treasure.

On the bench where he had taken his first post he places Agnes on his knee, and together they are frozen. People circle them. Hands reach forward to touch Agnes's skin, to verify that she, like them, is a living thing. She does not move. The crowd murmurs.

Where did he get the kid?

Should we do something?

That can't be safe, surely?

A blur of motion and pink flesh breaks from the mass; Argento turns his head an imperceptible fraction. Agnes is snatched from his hands.

What have you done, John? Patina says. What have you done?

Her voice crackles with tears.

Argento is pulled from the bench by a dissenter and he collapses onto the ground as though boneless. Others descend on him, a dark copse of kicking legs. Water is poured onto his face and another hand smears it, revealing the pale flesh underneath. Sirens come, red-and-blue lights reflected by his skin, and his persecutors scatter.

As they drag the statue towards the flashing car, he prays for the words to come. Those illuming words that will liberate him. That will have them fall to their knees, palms raised to him in supplication, painting themselves silver in his image. Without motion rejoicing.

In the white-lit room the detectives stare at him, waiting. His skin is pink, scrubbed raw.

Well, I've always liked the word, he tells them.

Statuary. Your mouth and tongue take on all manner of shapes when you say it. Do it now, he says, and they oblige. They shrug, unimpressed.

The rest is difficult to explain. The truth eludes even him.

The Commuter Town

Mark Ward

is possessive of its quiet,
turning in early. The winter nights
like a sedative. Babies, dogs
wake their parents when morning drapes itself
around the windows like a flasher
on a long exposure. The neighbourhood
WhatsApp threads are an endless stream
of warnings, pleading, backhands.
The city is too far away in a taxi. You are
too old for the night bus. A life
consumed by constant crying.
Having a child is a form of prayer: giving
oneself up to the hope of something greater.
A tiredness that prompts blood tests
but the results come back normal. Your child leaves.
Your other child leaves. You keep
the house presentable, your marriage.
You go to work, marking days like a guilty prisoner
due release. You plan a trip. Another. The children
never visit and the house demands a lived-in quiet,
a sacrifice of stillness which you can no longer
provide so you move to Spain, revelling in being
in someone else's space, becoming a nuisance,
a character. You sell the house to a young couple
expecting their first child.

Something Sharp

Enda Coyle-Greene

Her visit to the Other Queen
(at her place) a risk,

neither of them known to tiptoe,
stoop or even sneeze

with an apology, the Pirate takes
the proffered gift (nun-made

lace perhaps, or silk) blows
then throws it on the fire.

The other woman, younger
redhaired daughter

of a man prone to marriage
and a wife who lost her head,

(one of two from a full set of six)
so therefore, naturally, wary,

bridles at the Pirate, no stranger
to men, led or bedded,

who disposes who she pleases,
whenever she desires,

(rather in the manner of the Other
Queen's dead dad).

Lit by firelight, sole source of heat
in a (so far) chilly room,

there's a glinting hint of metal,
a shuffling of muscle

as her host exclaims her shock
at such a lack of manners.

Frisked on her way in, for a change
not armed with something

sharp, the Pirate parries, lunges
(just with words) to say that

where she's from, no one sheathes
their snot inside a sleeve,

or hides it in a pocket.

Karankawa

Éamon Ó Caoineachan

Many ancient Gaelic clans could walk in
water crossing a cold windy lough towards
wooded roundhouse island-homes – crannóg.
The key to unlocking this mystery
lies hidden below the surface
underwater – secret stepping stones ...

Yet as I stand on this Gulf Coast strand
over four thousand miles away from
crannógs in the middle of the sanded path
of Karankawa Beach Access Point #19
west of Galveston on Jamaica Beach
close by to an old Karankawa campsite
and burial ground now just a wayside historical
marker by roadside it lies stating they are 'now extinct'
when they are not. My elbows because I do not
know are sun-winged akimbo limbo.
I wonder why the Lipan Apache called
the coastal tribe the Karankawa 'Nda Kun dadehe'?
which translates to the 'people who walk in the water'.

Maybe the way they fished and caught turtles
with leaping foot waving hand-signs reflecting
the scales and the shells in bow and arrow eyes?
Maybe the way they surfed the waves-swell riding
waters well above turquoise sea below turquoise sky?
Maybe the way during the tide pull of moon-season
the turquoise sea moved in and out and in created deep parts
sandbar shallow shore making it appear they walked in
water? Or maybe miracle to this mystery?

I stand where the grey Lipan Apache
saw it and where their greyer horse neighed
in the high southern sunlight skimming steps –
bare bronze Karankawa feet rising and falling
like slow motion skipping stones and yet rising
up again – golden sunlight steps cast
shadows glow on the water-walkers star-feet
scaled fish in their hands and shelled turtles on their back
so wonderful striking the miracle of awe
there they are living up to their clan-name from afar

K a r a n k a w a
P e o p l e w h o w a l k i n t h e w a t e r.

The Far West

Denise McSheehy

WE ARRIVE LATE ONE SUMMER NIGHT. The key has been left under a pot round the back of the house. It's very quiet and the air soft. The back yard gritty underfoot and in the gulley for the drains water gleams like a black jewel.

There are three of us and we have three cats. A fourth cat to be sent down Red Star at a later date. The cat, Handel, had been reluctant to comply with the demands of train timetables and taken his regular constitutional regardless. A school friend of the daughters volunteers to take care of him and we discover afterwards that she has secured this vagrant and dishevelled cat in her bed to keep him safe. We are appalled, being familiar with his habit of flatulence and excessive dribbling.

Jago is one of the first neighbours to greet us.
'How do me'andsomes,' he says.
'Youse ladies want curtains up at them windows. Village centre like.' He winks.
'Oh,' I say, the daughters sniggering vilely. Jago is fiftyish and wears a suit jacket and stained trousers.
'My wife's dead,' he says.
'Oh,' I say, 'I'm so sorry.'
'Hung herself in front room there.'
Terrible images flash into our heads. Traffic roars through the village, hundreds of cars a day despite the bypass. Jago's house abuts the street, the front window obscured by dirty nets. We think of Jago's wife, her feet just a

little way off the floor. A brief lull in the traffic.

I am sweet to Jago of course. In a kind neighbourly sort of way and in view of his bereavement. He spends a good deal of time in the King's Head just across the road from us in the square. A very popular drinking haunt with the locals who favour bringing their pints over to our porch to hang out. One evening, shortly after we move in, we return from Truro to find a dozen or so men lounging outside the window and against the front door. Our parking space is on the cobbles in front of the house and we are allowed grudging access.
'Excuse me,' I say, the daughters crowding behind me timorously as we go in.

The next week Jago presents at the front door to invite me out.
'Well I'm still unpacking, Jago,' I say, 'It's very nice of you. Maybe another time.'
Jago is not slow and knows when he's been rejected.

Handel arrives later that week in a box. We collect him at the station. His joy visible as we extricate him smelly and dribbling from his transport. The cats settle in and slaughter a rat in the garden shed with a slash across the throat. I find it stretched dramatically across the threshold.

We are really in the centre of things here. Everything happens in the square and has done for the last 200 years according to the village annals. Ears cut off, fisticuffs and so forth. Our cottage is number 2. The Happy Shopper being number 1.

A loud crunch and we come out to find a jeep jammed in the wall of the shop. One of the local farmers has a drink problem. Known in the area as a dastardly individual currently engaged in proceedings with the RSPCA concerning the state of his cows. He reverses away from the wall and The Happy Shopper staff count their losses.

Another evening one of the local men, part of the group who hang around outside our house (they are all men rather than boys, married with small children when we spot them out with the wife on Saturday mornings) – chucks a brick through the shop window. Glass everywhere, lots of shouting. No-one knows what he's on about. The local police arrive, six of them, and they sit on the offender. A stocky mild character during the day but with a shot of alcohol inside him turns into an uncontrollable octopus of a man, writhing and bawling and weeping in the middle of the road.

The sound of gun-fire. I open the front door. Smoke hangs in the air. The King's Head drinkers, those from inside as well as outside, are all out on the square, muttering and whispering, shifting uncomfortably, heads up questioning.
'Did someone fire a gun?'
More indistinguishable muttering – an unwillingness to break ranks. I have daughters and must take responsibility.
'Has anyone called the police?'
General ignorance is expressed. I make the call.
The woman with the gun has retreated – a neighbour just up the lane from us. We hear subsequently she is suffering from post-natal depression and driven to madness by the raucous shouts from the King's Head drinkers who convene outside her house as well.

'I did see a woman with a rifle go past the window,' a daughter says conversationally later. She has been sitting at the kitchen table doing her homework. The kitchen window looks onto the pedestrian lane from low down. She must have seen the rifle at face level as it advanced.
'And you didn't think to say anything?' I ask. Mildly.
'Well no. It's Cornwall.'

Village life in the far west. Disconcertingly eccentric; but we are charmed. The long way down feeling of the peninsula. Lowering skies suddenly clearing late afternoon, the wash of white. The sea's salt presence even far inland. Engine houses and a smoky blue haze of heather along the clifftops.

Like the cats we settle in. And it's the house that charms us too. The front rather formal and eighteenth century, the back cottagey with a bulging wall and deep windows. Inside it's womb-like, particularly the kitchen which has an old range I stoke with anthracite. The stairs to the half landing, carpeted in an ancient green fabric, suggest a Bonnard painting – exuding warmth and intimacy.

The day my mother dies the house fills with a golden sleepy afternoon light.

Sun reaching all windows on the west side like a blessing. Late August, in the heart of the house it is still.

The daughters grow and stomp around in their Doc Martins and sit exams and hitch across the county to support local bands of teenage boys. I find a corner of the house in which to write. Crab apples fall in the slow hot garden, splitting and seething under a net of flies.

The Door

Alexander Etheridge

for Olav H. Hauge

It's October here
where second by second
I lose the entire
world, and gain it back again.
Is this the way it was
meant to be – such gifts
and such grief?

While I sit and stare,
the cottonwoods
all around me keep their
wings up
over red and delicate
wild berries, rust-coloured
brambles, and scattered lemon leaves.
The heart of the earth

is untroubled and calm
like a hidden pond
between nightbreezes.
I want the words

that will give me up to
the silent mind of
autumn, maybe one word,
my last thought

like a door opening

into the cool orchards
I dreamt of long ago.

Scavenged

Jamie O'Halloran

Yesterday, I saw a beauty,
      a piece of tree laying against
            the hedgerow. Barkless

and bleached, more like a find along
      the strand, not thrown
            down by a winter storm.

I picked it up. Its dearth of weight
      surprised me, airy,
            a mass of atoms tumbling

through ether. On the floor beside
      the grate it changes from branch
            into something other than tree,

with a bend in it much like
      a knee or elbow. I make it
            the heart of this early fire

expanding to fill the hearth.
        Crooked fuel, I have to feed
              the embers into flames again

with the driest kindling, reedy
        branches of hydrangea. Its joint chars
              into a carbon frown, mouth seared

by fiery licks as the once-tree shifts into vapour.
        What I stole now steals breath –
              Heat-giver I took for a gift.

To an Old Friend

Kevin Graham

1.

I hadn't thought of you in a while,
the train having left the station
to take in births and deaths and stall
in little moments of confusion.
Your prognosis came as a surprise –
how could it not – the mind falling
back to when we were teenagers
on the brow of a hill overlooking
the sea in our school uniforms.
A string of drool linked our chaste lips
which you brushed away casually,
laughing at the absurd passion of youth
and talking nonchalantly
about important things like truth.

2.

I don't know what it means and can
only imagine. The relationship
to eternity must be a kinship
from birth or a visiting dysfunction
from childhood. What is the aetiology
of love? Mornings I'd wake like a fuse
picturing you and your harmony
with the world. Why do we choose
each other out of all the others?
Something compels us, as in a river,
threading through the places
we haven't been. Is it ever really over?
I'm thinking of you now
the way a sky might think of snow.

In the time it takes

Marc Swan

for eggs to sizzle in melted butter
a great blue heron drops
low beyond the river bank
with a steady glide
like the wings of a jet
soaring high above a strip of land
where ordinary people live –
dropping leaflets one day,
explosives the next, and so it goes
from one troubled spot to another –
the power of misunderstanding
breeding chaos, confusion, despair
to those who rise in the morning,
put the kettle on, get children
ready for school, kiss one another
at the door, not realising in places
of unrelenting sorrow
a kiss may be their sayonara

Boa Constrictor

Lisa C. Taylor

IT WASN'T JUST THE BOA CONSTRICTOR bedecked with daisies tattoo that unnerved me. Twelve names of women wound around his arm from hand to shoulder: Bree, Dahlia, Corine, Bitty, Sedona, Ida, Sasha, Derry, Nora, Cally, Cait, Poof. I was fixated on Bitty and Poof. What kind of names are those? Were they women or pets? Could they be nicknames, like Bitty for a small woman and Poof for a wild-haired lady?

When Campbell asked me to take a walk with him on a steamy day in early September, I said yes. He showed up in a grey muscle shirt with all his body art exposed. I thought of needles and inks and the kind of pain tolerance and patience it takes to sit for someone to permanently decorate your body. I don't get it and I don't like it. Tattoos are like a body deformity I can't unsee. A woman in my yoga class had a big puffy brown mole above her lip. I wanted to drop her the name of a doctor who could slice it off for her, surely an outpatient procedure that would not cost much. God, I'd even pay for it if it meant I didn't have to look at that thing.

Campbell is friendly, reserved even. He tells me about his daughter, Kalia. She's five and lives mostly with her mother. Apparently, her name wasn't important enough to make it to the mural on his arm. Who were these women? I construct the beginnings of conversations.

'How's Derry? Is she still lactose intolerant?'

'I heard Poof had her hair straightened and now she's called Chic.'

Unless these are relatives or pets who died, it is creepy to carry around a lifetime tribute. It's kind of like stalking, isn't it? I would not want my name on my ex's arm, leg, shoulder, or any other body part. What happens when you're in bed?

'Is Morgan your mom or grandma?'

'No, she was my ex but I never got over her.'

'Oh shit, call from work. Got to go. Sorry.'

And the postscript: I'll text you … ever.

Campbell has the demeanour of an accountant who attends church every Sunday paired with the body of a motorcycle dude. He tells me he's buying a house, put a down deposit on a small ranch next to the elementary school. Kalia can walk there when she's not at her mom's.

I wonder if I can ask him to wear long-sleeved shirts, even in bed. Is it a deal breaker? Campbell is the first in what I'd consider a long dry spell – like two years. There was the pandemic and then I was suspicious of everyone. We all breathe and talk and that was off the table. The pandemic times are now the cautious maybe times. Covid is still here but less lethal, especially for younger people. Everyone I know has been infected and they all survived, though my granny got long Covid and is still tired and a little confused.

My internal monitor likes Campbell. He's funny and approachable, has a decent body.

My friend Torie texts me.

What happened?

So many tattoos

lmao

Names of ladies

Ick

Right?

Am I seeking validation that one should never seriously consider a dude with tattoos? The pool of single men in their thirties or forties *without* tattoos is shrinking. Should I ask them to strip on a first date to verify? That seems forward.

Campbell texts me.

Stargazing tonight? I'll bring beer.

I hate beer but I like stargazing. I hate tattoos but I like Campbell.

Sure. When?

We set the time and place and I tell him I don't drink beer but like wine. He is accommodating.

Everyone has a story but most of us don't write it on our bodies. I carry a tiny gold acorn when I travel, a gift from my sister, Maura. Morgan and Maura. We were practically twins even though we were sixteen months apart. We even looked alike with our reddish-brown hair and prominent eyebrows. Maura was an inch shorter than me and way better in science and math. She wanted to be a scientist or a doctor but that did not happen. She never had a chance to have a serious partner or finish college. Half of me lives in a world I can't see or touch. Maura still exists somewhere; I'm convinced of that. I'm not allowed into her realm and I have no eyes or capacity to understand or see into the void. I did not get a tattoo of her name but I have the acorn and a small Claddagh ring she gave me for my sixteenth birthday.

Okay, Campbell. I'll play. Maybe the daisies disarm the boa constrictor. I've never liked snakes but flowers make everything more tolerable.

It is getting dark earlier. We meet outside Dabney Park. There's a hill where lots of people go sledding in winter and stargaze in summer. Because it's cooler tonight, there is no one else here. Campbell lays down a plaid blanket and unpacks a bottle of wine, real glasses, and a package of chocolate-dipped biscuits. He is wearing a long-sleeved striped button-down.

'Wine?' He flourishes a corkscrew.

'Sure,' I say, though I'm not sure about anything.

The stars are showing off, blinking like some crazy firework display or those stupid strobe-like Christmas lights. We lie on our backs and he points out the constellations. I mean, he's ticking all the boxes except the one that says *no piercings or tattoos*. Torie tells me to be flexible. I tell her to stop dating losers who eat all her food and can't stay employed. She says I'm right but falls for the wrong man over and over.

There is an art to finding a partner. I do not know it.

Campbell leans over and kisses me, gently at first, and then with passion. I fold into him and for a moment, I'm a part of the stars and Maura is there with some quip and a blunt. I'm having an existential moment.

'Why a boa constrictor?' I ask, resting on my elbows.

'Y'know how life sometimes squeezes you?'

I nod though I have no idea what he is talking about.

He goes on.

'Impermanence, death ... like spring lilacs that bloom for such a short time'

'But daisies go on all summer.'

'Yeah. Badass. I like that.'

I'm still not getting it but his arm is around me and he's leaning in for another kiss.

I have lots of restrictions: no smokers, stoners, heavy drinkers, men who are rude or crude. I hate gum-chewing or tobacco-spitting. Campbell does not seem to be any of those things.

After the kind of kiss that feels sexy without a tongue down my throat, he tells me about the women.

'Cait was Kalia's twin. She didn't make it. We had a list of names for her. We called her Itty-bitty and Poof because she had this fluff on top of her head. She lived four days.'

I tell him about Maura, how she was not a twin but like a twin. It's almost an amputation or maybe the removal of an internal organ. The shadow of completeness is still there but it's just a whisper. I've never told anyone but Torie how she died but I tell Campbell about the man who shot her at a concert that our parents didn't want her to attend. Random shooting, the police said. Wrong place, wrong time. What would be the right place and the right time? Earlier that day, she was looking for a prom dress, had a clipping from an online ad printed. We were both going to wear teal. It was her senior prom and my junior prom. I bought a black dress instead of a prom gown and went to the saddest funeral anyone could imagine.

Cait was a four-day-old infant. Maura was an eighteen-year-old adult, headed to Penn State to study science.

We stay tangled on the hill for what seems like hours. Finally Campbell extricates his arm and kisses me on the forehead.

'Can I see you again?' As if that question had more than one answer.

I don't know why I hate tattoos. Maybe it's because I don't want to invite pain. Women suffer during childbirth and suffer again if anything happens to their kids. My mother lost a lot of weight after Maura died. They had to sit through hours of questioning and video footage. The shooter killed himself at the scene so senseless violence had no consequence except unfathomable loss.

Sometimes I dream about Maura. She's a doctor now, pregnant with her first child. We meet up in beachy places like Ireland, Newport Beach, and Chincoteague Island. I like her husband and I know she'll like Campbell. After her son is born we plan to buy houses in the same town.

There is a life beyond this life. It's not reincarnation or rebirth. I don't have a name for it but I know it's there. In that life, Maura got to have a first love, take classes to learn what she most wanted to learn. In that life, it is possible to stay whole.

Barking the Sails

Stephen de Búrca

Rising and falling arrhythmically, our ferry
travels to Inishmore. At the bow, I watch
a wind turbine scythe clockwise on the edge

of the mainland. White in the fog, it is at odds
with the hooker etching spirals on the sea.
With neither boom nor stays, it is a púcán –
the smallest of those Galway hookers, those

workhorses of the west that lugged turf out,
poitín and limestone slabs by return. Its sails
are well and truly barked – the yearly treatments
of tar and butter have weatherproofed their red

to russet. Sharing names with lore's shape-shifter,
foregrounded now by the turbine, it is passed
by us on the ferry and I follow it
to stern. The water churns away with more

at stake these warmer days and I watch the old
and new dissolve in the Atlantic fret,
sloshed by the smell of diesel.

We all had a colour in that house –

Maria Isakova Bennett

Prussian blue for my father
and his father – the long journey

east to west; my auntie, a room alone
with clockwork music boxes, umber

for autumn; my mother reduced
to beige or grey, some mud in the mix

until she escaped and became
a summer-palette to flood scarves;

my brother black and white, lines
and geometry full of measured space;

my sisters both pinks of Angel Delight,
false but vivid, became something teal;

and me? Whatever they decided –
girl in tidy-reds, collar buttoned up,

until I had choice, which came
after winters, mourning on mourning,

my attempt at any and all greens –
sap, verdigris, apple, olive.

Mother, Nature

Sai Liuko

My mother, elbow-deep in soil, again
tries to pry open my pit. I watch her moving through the shadow-
striped foliage,

not bothering to say something about windows, subtle signs. Because
she leaves them lightless. Misunderstands

how surely a tree is a family with soft undergrowth.
The alocasia is drooping, the evergreens

watered but rarely nourished. The verdure
for her, a witness of her nature,

not of a will to preserve selves. (When I
am drowning she is on fire.)

You have let the green aerate you but do
not realise your role as lungs, I said,

that time on that walk, dead of winter:
Root rot, I said. I love you, she said.

The sprouting system truly a meat-eating
flower we couldn't germinate. Only

the excuses took seed, mycelial, in me,
and there was no forgiving. But

when she lies down in her green sheet dress,
neck-deep between the moss, I know that

I have just failed to learn that a cutting can
save a living thing, despite whatever sweet nectar

oozed out. After all those years, I have built a
sunroom.

Leeches

Luke Morgan

They fall from the sky here, we're told,
climbing through trees to the leprosy hospital
where knobbled clay and painted blinds
spell the miles from Galway like heat from cold.
On our phones is a video by our cameraman, full
of giddy horror at a gentle leech he finds

near his heel. The picture wobbles as he tips
salt onto its back. A few moments of calm
where you wonder if the salt thing is just a myth
before blood blooms from its lips,
bursting slow like ink from a dam,
appalling all back home we share it with.

A doctor gives us the tour. Patients smile and namaste,
press fists together for the Westerners,
not knowing why we're here, or caring;
it's lunch hour and they're getting on with their day,
demonstrating balled stumps when he refers
to them in English, numb to our staring.

We're here to make a film, raise vital funds.
Half of us try and blend in by ditching shoes
(which is how we were found by our famous leech).
We'll gather our footage, swap our suns,
spread awareness of this place, choose
to believe all we regurgitate is speech.

The Clearing

Natalie Rice

Winter, the wood is hard
and dry and when the moon rises,
a man bends to cut birch

saplings to stake a ring
for the spring garden. Sleep
has become starry, a brown jug heavy

with dried bulbs and roots, the air taken
in mouthfuls. In this round room
made from fieldstone and hemlock,
his only secrets are that once

he found himself in the body
of a five-hundred-year-old
fox, and that he needs the clear night
of being alone. After the cut

he stands to listen as a frozen
pond does. When he walks back
to the house, his pail swings against
the white fields, the white stones
under snow.

Forty-One Degrees North, Forty-Nine Degrees West

John O'Donnell

ON DAYS WHEN RAIN COMES PELTING DOWN he watches through the window as the river rises, his breath ghosting the glass. When the Casla bursts her banks there are always stories: a black cat, unmoored, clinging to a floating kitchen stool, a rag doll hurtling downstream towards the ocean. He limps more heavily on days like these; the doctor warns him that the diabetes is advancing, that he may lose the leg. But he knows the surgeon's saw will not avail him, that what afflicts him will still be there.

A flotilla of torn branches sluices past the back wall of the garden. The house is set well back from the road, hidden carefully by tall trees. 'Our wild and solitary place,' his wife calls it, and it is as far as it is possible to imagine from the leafy squares of London, the city's fogs and evasions, the hostile glances and boardroom silences, the empty spaces either side of him at the club table. How well she knows him, to have understood that this is where he might even be happy; standing mid-river, the Casla in full spate, brown water streaming past him as he casts his line.

The river teems with fish. Brown trout, rainbow trout; salmon especially, an embarrassment of salmon, so many that you could almost reach down into the cold depths and scoop one out by hand, a wriggling slippery life. Last season they caught over three hundred of them; they ended up feeding them to the dogs. In summer, if the day is fine, he goes out on the rowing boat. She is sturdy, clinker-built, with plenty of room for tackle and fish-boxes and blankets. Occasionally the two boys go with him: Thomas, when he comes to visit, and young George. He is a worrier, George, his knuckles whitening as he grips the thwart-seat, his chin tucked in against his life-vest. 'I don't like this,' the boy whines, and when he reassures his youngest son that he is perfectly safe, he can see Micheál, the local man who minds the boat, looking away, eyes fixed astern as he hauls steadily on the oars. 'That's far enough, Micheál,' he says when they reach the mouth of the river, and the man stops rowing and begins to scull the boat around.

The river yes, but not the sea. Not anymore.

Rosmuc, Carraroe, Inverin, Rossaveal. The names sound like snatches of tunes. He will never understand this language that they speak, the men murmuring to each other at the end of a day's fishing as they follow behind him, carrying the boxes of gleaming silver back to the house. He rewards them generously, a couple of salmon each, as well as what he pays them. It is good business to keep them loyal, and he is good at business, like his father. Rivets, funnels, boilers, girders: he can quickly assess the likely cost and then offer a good price; it's a skill that he is proud of. But no corners cut. What he builds is by the book, in full compliance with all the regulations. 'I was *exonerated*,' he wails, waking in the night to find the house at sea, a widowed shutter banging in the furious gale; and when he is like this she holds him and strokes his hair, waiting for him to return.

On Sundays the two of them drive to Screeb. The roads are little more than dirt tracks. They pass walls of silent stone, and wizened fairy thorns that squint into the wind. The chapel is surprisingly full. 'Soupers,' the locals call those other locals behind their backs, the ones who switched their faith to save their skins. The vicar is fretful: there has been one Great War already, but there is talk now of another, and he calls upon the Lord to bless the minds of those involved, that they may be inspired to do the right thing. He sits up front beside his wife, he sings the hymns and bows his head, half-listening as the clergyman intones the names of all those in the parish who have recently passed away: the Altar List of the Dead.

And – a curious eccentricity, he realises this – on Sundays he will not allow the men to accompany him on the river unless they have first been to Mass. The men redden when he asks, busying themselves with rods and lines at the little pier behind the house: *what business is it of his*? But he insists, and sometimes he quotes the Psalms: *They that go down to the sea in ships, these men see the work of the Lord.* The doctor comes out fishing with him sometimes, watching uneasily as he manoeuvres himself into the boat. Once or twice the parish priest comes as well, a further gesture of generosity, the priest laughing as he takes a swig from the proffered flask. There are days when he feels blessed, sunlight dappling the river, water clucking against the hull. Golden Olive, Pheasant Tail, Claret Dabbler, Silver Rat: the chosen fly is attached neatly to the line he casts, a silk thread looping through the air until it lands, touching the water above the rock where legend says the big fish hide. And when one rises and snatches at the hidden hook, he can lose himself in the contest, the reel whirring as the line is wound in, and then paid out, and wound in again until the creature finally succumbs and is lifted in the landing net.

Another list: one of the American newspapers, after the inquiry, stoking public rage on both sides of the Atlantic. A full page, divided into two. In one section, every single name, row by row by row, over fifteen hundred of them. And in the other section, one name only; his own.

He is grateful to her; she does her best. She visits the local school each time they come to stay, bringing with her bags of sweets shipped specially from Manhattan. The children fall on them with delight, the wrappings that they come in as intriguing as the sweets themselves. How she misses New York, the city of her birth; those impossibly tall buildings, the clamorous streets, the endless pulsing life. And yet she realises that they – that he – never can return there.

'Coward'.

In the house at Casla she has a rule, the same rule that she has in London; the rule is that it is never mentioned, not by staff, not by guests, not even by the children. At Christmastime there are presents, scarves and trinkets for the women in the kitchen and the laundry-room, and for the men who work the river there is for each of them a goose, its innards stuffed with a bottle of poteen. Each year he hosts a party in the house, the sideboards and tables lavished with grapefruits, bananas, pears. There is music; a piano, which she plays, and the instruments the locals bring, fiddles, bodhráns, whistles, which they later cradle in their laps as they sing unaccompanied their songs of far-eyed sadness, of love gone wrong, young lives destroyed. Sometimes on these nights as the whiskey settles in his bones he sees the slanting deck, littered with chips of ice, the radio operator still frantically tapping out the ship's location; he sees the passengers from First Class, standing in coats and dressing-gowns, their faces filled not with fear but disbelief. How long did he spend hoisting the rumps of those well-upholstered women and their shivering children up over the rail into the boats? And he'd insisted they take everyone, everyone he could find: *Move over there! Squeeze up! You can fit another, surely!*

He'd made certain that every single boat was filled, until the entire starboard deck was empty, not a soul left standing on the frosty promenade. Except him. 'What more could I have done?' he asks the darkness when he wakens suddenly, her sleeping form beside him. But he will never find forgiveness in this place, where rain is second nature, the waters rising, fields becoming lakes, the land going under, sinking.

During the final summer he can barely stand. He sleeps more and more. The morphine dulls the pain but clouds his mind: he hears voices, or thinks he does, whisperings on the corridors, the stairs, the younger women, giggling. '*Shee-as May.*' Is this the opiate haze the doctor warned of, or are they calling to him in their language, his name 'Mr Ismay' now becoming 'Mr Síos Mé'? His grip loosens. He has lost his bearings: what are the co-ordinates for this, the longitude and latitude of a life?

In London he lies slumped in a wheelchair. A high window gives out onto the street; he can hear cars and lorries, footsteps passing on the pavement, the city's ebb and flow. October; the Casla is closed for fishing, the season over. He tries to summon up a far-off afternoon, standing in the river, rod in hand, ready to cast. But the image will not come; he cannot even lift his wrist. His eyes roll over the stump of his left leg. The rest of him is frozen; the stroke after the surgery has done its work, or almost, since he is still here. In the dying autumn light his eyes swivel towards the heavens and then close; he is praying for salvation, for a vessel that might somehow be lowered from above to rescue him. To take him down.

He takes a step towards the guardrail. The top edge of the last collapsible is already level with the deck. As he clambers over, one of the slippers he is wearing goes from under him; he stumbles, clinging for a moment to the rail before he lands inside the lifeboat, falling awkwardly against a large man in a bowtie. One of the crewmen works the ropes; the other is on his feet, fending off as they descend, the canvas sides bumping against the hull.

When they touch down on the water's surface the boat barely makes a splash. The sea is like black glass; there is no moon, but there are stars, hundreds of them, crowding overhead in the night sky.

Immediately the two crewmen begin to row.

There are two spare oars left. 'Well, no point waiting around, I guess,' says the man in the bowtie, seizing one of the oars. American.

The other oar is still lying there; he picks it up and starts rowing.

They come upon a young man bobbing in a life-vest; already his face is blue. 'Please,' he says, his hand reaching up, curling over the gunwale. The boat begins to rock, water sloshing in over the sides.

'We can't,' a woman says, 'we're full.'

'Please,' the young man says again, though he is tiring.

The American stands up, lifting his oar out of the water. 'Let go, you fool, you'll kill us all,' he says, and he brings the oar down on the young man's fingers. The boat shudders at the blow.

They begin to row again. The women in the stern are looking at him, their verdict clear. Behind them the ship by now is almost vertical; there is a series of whumps and pops and blasts and then she disappears, the sea closing over the lights of a lost world. On and on they go in the starlit darkness, until the only sound he can hear is the dip and pull of the oars cutting through water, and the glittering droplets falling from the blades.

The Dance

Ciarán O'Rourke

Pieter Bruegel, 1568

First summer flush, the growing fields afloat
in blue and garnered green.

The far-off borders
buckle, at the deathly Duke's advance –

though merry morning still can make a mark,
as the piper, frowsy, rumbles up a reel,

the village dancers thump and spin.
All about, the climbing birches glisten,

their shifting, whispered canopy a-gleam.
The intimate intricacies prevail.

Sitting close, in motley muck, a hunkered
watcher wheezes at the rim, relieved.

Two hatted passers hail the swirling set.
On a rocky mount, in words of wind,

the craning gallows croak for joy! Seated
at the base and beam, a vigilating magpie.

Room to Breathe

Leen Raats

And then everything suddenly seems to fall into place
like a puzzle that has been lying
on the table for many months, untouched.

How you find space here to breathe
among pollard willows who, like stubborn peasants
with their hands in their pockets, lean against the wind.

A place you've never been before, but that feels familiar
like a song you recognise from the first time you hear it.

How you do not desire more than what you are,
your eyes following crows in their flight.

The murmur of a city in the distance. And the wind
who seeks itself in the tree tops.

You stretch out like a slow summer evening
that does not fall but always has been.

Summer '76

Sara Mullen

In sunglasses
and rolled-up sleeves,
the adults lounged,

their conversation
far away, humming
with the bees.

The back garden
a rampage of roses
and ripe blackcurrants.

You marooned
on the blue island of
your comfort blanket,

in a white sunhat
too small for your head.
Your first summer;

my fourth, flaunting
an orange bikini, a
plastic basin for my pool.

Called over for
a photograph with you,
the first baby

ever handed to me
to hold. The closest
we ever were, that day.

Sunshine would wane
and the last blue shreds
of your blanket fade and scatter.

Argos Dreamed

Linda Opyr

An incessant twitch, the sudden kick.
For twenty years, Argos cried in dreams.

The nightly clash of swords on starless shores.
A spear and the hot smell of blood stinking foreign sand.

Footsteps of strangers across wine-spilled floors.
A boast. A dare. Greed and lust dipping their bread.

The secrecy of despair: woman's work.
Weaving by day. Scheming by dark.

And always the heave of a heavy sea.
The breaker crash of crew taken.

Wind. Tide. This god, that.
The final creaking of cavernous ship.

Argos swung his tail side to side.
Whimpered his rheumy eyes shut.

A distant war. So very far.
So very close. Still.

A Man Who Must Be Listened To

Steve Wade

TOO BLEEDING COLD TO STINK *like hell* Alex Clifford said to himself, as he stopped to watch a couple of swans drift beneath the bridge and disappear.

He half wondered how long a body could survive were it to find itself in the freezing waters below. Before the end of the week, he'd be in a position to find out.

With his guitar case hanging from his shoulder, Alex's thoughts returned to the song. Now there was a song that deserved all the praise, national and international, that had been heaped upon it. If only he could source the inspiration to write such a song. That surely would bring him the fame he craved.

For Alex, only when you had innate talent and put in the workload, the time and effort, did you truly deserve fame. Sickly as a child, he'd spent a lot of time out of school. But those days he didn't squander. He put in thousands of hours of practice on the six- and twelve-string guitar.

He wrote his own songs too. He even had a couple of them recorded by a singer who was almost a household name. A regular doing gigs in a few pubs and a support act at small music festivals gave him the courage to walk away from his riveting civil service job. Audiences loved him. He'd received accolades in local and national media, but he could never quite get the exposure he knew would gain him the attention he warranted.

He arrived at his usual busking spot and set himself up.

He was landing on the one-word chorus of Leonard Cohen's most enduring song, when some young old guy with a prematurely grey beard stopped before him. With him on the end of what looked like a length of frayed parcel twine, a red, terrier-type dog, greying about the muzzle like its owner. Alex watched as he tied the dog's makeshift lead to a bike rack.

Swaddled in a dirty grey and blue sleeping bag, the beard stepped in close to Alex and reached out a hand with long, filthy fingernails. Alex twisted his guitar away from him. Through his scruffy reddish grey beard, the guy wore a permanent smile. He stepped backward, turned sideways to the crowd, closed his eyes, and snarled a gravely 'Hallelujah', his head swinging from side to side.

'My new singing partner,' Alex said to the crowd, which got a few titters. 'Hallelujah,' he sang. 'We've been working together now for –' he paused for effect – 'oh fifteen seconds. Hallelujah.' A bigger laugh came from the crowd. And then the street guy did something which drew hoots of approval from those gathered. He shucked off the sleeping bag from around his shoulders in a stylish manner that seemed practised. Leaving it where he tossed it on the ground, he then proceeded to act out or convey the words of the song using gestures, mime and facial expressions as Alex sang.

Before a fresh verse, Alex invited the street guy to step forward to the mic and introduce himself. As though awaiting this cue, the beard skipped towards him, put his hairy face too close to the microphone and spoke in a voice that sounded like cracked granite.

'The Growler,' he said. He pointed to his dog. 'And his name is Rags.' He stepped backwards.

More laughter from the crowd.

'Fair fucks to you, Mr Growler,' a man's voice shouted from the street audience.

Back into the zone, Alex sang a line in the song that tells the listener the songwriter had done his best. The Growler made a wide-eyed, determined expression and shook his clenched fist, his face twisting into a Charlie Chaplin sad-eyed look to convey how ineffective L. Cohen felt his efforts had been.

A ripple of applause wove through the crowd but died away to hear more clearly Alex singing about being unable to *feel* and his attempt to *touch*. This his unkempt partner got across by wrapping his arms about his own shoulders and then moving balletically to his dog, where he'd tied it to the bike rack. He stretched out his arm, just beyond the terrier's reach at the end of the lead. Rags barked and pulled on the twine.

A yelp of appreciation from the crowd was followed by a whistle, one somebody made with two fingers in their mouth.

In the last lines of the stanza, Alex felt, through the timbre in his own voice, he alighted on something he had never achieved. Without consciously striving to do so, he straightened to his fullest height, as did his new friend. And while his backup dancer craned his head backwards, his eyes shut, his arms above his head to embrace the *Lord of Song*, Alex, likewise, leaned back his head as the whole crowd gathered around him sang the chorus twice.

The applause and cheers of the crowd was like nothing Alex had ever experienced. If those gathered weren't already on their feet, they'd be giving them a standing ovation.

The Growler shifted about among the dispersing crowd, the filthy white baseball cap removed from his head and pushed beneath their noses. He badgered a few of them until they reluctantly put their hands in their pockets.

'There you go, Boss,' the Growler said as he tipped the coins and notes he'd collected into Alex's hard-shell guitar case.

In normal times Alex would have got himself to a quiet table in a café, where he could count his takings. But as there was nowhere open to have indoor refreshments, he ordered a couple of takeout pizzas and coffees. They then headed for the city's central park. In a relatively quiet spot Alex shifted about to ensure he was upwind of the Growler.

Before taking a bite from his pepperoni pizza, he opened his guitar case, lifted the guitar by the neck and took out the green cloth bag from the inner compartment. From the bag, without counting them, he separated a fistful of coins from the notes and handed them to the Growler. About thirty or forty euro at a glance and by the weight. The Growler, his eyes locked to Alex's hand, received them in his two manky hands held out and cupped together.

'Ah thanks, Boss. Thanks very much,' the Growler said, his permanent smile displaying yellowed teeth with a curious brown line that looked like it could have been painted across his upper ones.

'No. Thank you, buddy.'

'From rags to riches,' the Growler said, tearing off a slice of his own pizza and feeding it to his dog, Rags.

Alex arranged that the Growler join up with him a few more times that week. But when their appearance began to lose some of its surprise impact on their third outdoor gig, Alex arranged that they shift to a different part of town over the weekend.

Apart from pulling in more money than he ever had, Alex realised that maybe this partnership might just be what he needed to gain the publicity he deserved. A few surreptitious messages to a few local newspapers about the novelty busking act on the city's streets resulted only in some student rag publishing an article which focused on the Growler, with his dancing photo inset.

Alex put aside his creative prowess for writing songs one evening to concentrate on how the Growler might yet be the ship on which he set sail to the promised land of major outdoor gigs. His name headlining the bill. He sat down in his improvised studio at the kitchen table. A tingling sensation went down his spine as a choreographed group of ragged dancers in his head morphed into a flash mob, images of Michael Jackson's video to *Thriller* weaving their way into the idea. He teased out more possibilities, taking notes on ones that even seemed ridiculous, until, finally, the elusive something he'd been pursuing came to him like a perfect melody. Simple yet sublime.

Unseasonably mild on the day Alex and the Growler met up in a side alley to go over the plan, the Growler introduced him to his accomplice. As skinny as he was tall, the Growler's ashen-faced buddy regarded Alex through half-lidded eyes as he went over the plan.

'Is he getting this?' Alex asked the Growler about his pal.

'Aw yeah, sound,' the Growler said. 'No worries.'

'Right,' Alex said. Just don't fuck this up, lads, all right?'

'Sound,' the Growler said.

Alex shifted his attention to the tall guy. The Growler nudged him.

'Game ball,' he said. 'Sound.'

Alex twisted his wrist to glance at his watch and told them ten minutes. He left the ragged duo and made his way to the bridge that led to the city's main thoroughfare.

On cue, the Growler, his pal and Rags arrived. As though their purpose was far more important than those driving cars, buses, and trucks, the pair crossed at the lights when they were red for pedestrians. Car horns were held down and somebody shouted that they *get off the fucking road.*

On the bridge, the two started up what sounded like a growling match. Alex watched the plan unfold as he had outlined it. To a collective gasp of some passers-by, the Growler's pal snatched up the dog and tossed him over the bridge into the river. Roaring and shouting like a madman, the Growler clambered up onto the bridge wall and fell gracelessly more than the planned jump into the snot-green waters below.

With his newly purchased wetsuit on beneath his tracksuit, Alex didn't hesitate in pushing himself atop the bridge wall and plunging into the river. Something he regretted in a nanosecond. The Arctic bitterness of the water enveloped him as though he was vacuum packed in a skin of ice.

Gone now his vision of swimming, Tarzan-like, with his head and chest above the surface towards the drowning Growler and his dog. No images were there before him of the cheering and applauding crowd on the bridge above as he swam with his arm hooked about the Growler's neck bringing him to safety. In the arms of the Growler, Rags. No frontpage story would there be in the broadsheets and the tabloids accompanying photos of the heroic up-and-coming singer-songwriter selflessly *risking life and limb* to rescue the homeless man and his four-legged companion.

His head now above water, Alex tried, in vain, to wave his arms and move his legs. His body no longer worked. Paralysed.

Alex's last conscious memory before they got him to hospital was of the lava-like burning sensation in his lungs when his rescuers pulled him in to the quay walls. And the vomiting. He remembered the vomiting.

Hypothermia and cardiac arrest. Those were the two things Alex escaped by wearing a wetsuit beneath his clothes. One young male nurse said there might be a police inquiry into the incident, and they'd be around to talk to him now that he was fully conscious.

'And the Growler?' Alex asked him.

'What?' the Asian nurse said. 'How do you mean, sir?'

'The chap that jumped into the river. The one with the dog?'

The nurse told him to hold on. He left the ward and returned with a newspaper.

Alex read the headline. Homeless man survives drowning waters by clinging to bridge.

He scanned the article for any mention of his own daring efforts. Nothing. Until he homed in on the paragraph about the drowned dog. And how its owner, known by his fellow street people as the Growler, was too shocked and upset on the day to talk about his life on the streets with Rags. And, in particular, about the passer-by witnesses had seen jumping in after him in a failed rescue attempt. The article closed with the columnist insinuating that here was a story waiting to be told. The Growler, a man who must be listened to.

The Crannóg Questionnaire

Susan Isla Tepper

How would you introduce yourself as a writer to those who may not know you?

I would say that I'm a woman who is very alert to the world. Which is both a blessing and a curse, in that I can become obsessed with certain inequities and often become despairing. I think that particular quality in me is what drove me to become a writer. I started as an actress while in my teens, but abandoned it after several decades. For the past twenty or so years I've been writing steadily, producing eleven published books of fiction and poetry. Now I've turned back to theatre and I've written five plays. The first play to receive any recognition was titled *The Crooked Heart* and had a staged-reading at the Irish Repertory Theatre, in NYC, autumn of '22. The mainstage was packed and I was utterly entranced watching two great actors perform my words.

When did you start writing?

Officially, twenty or so years ago. But I actually wrote a poem while I was in my twenties, and still working as a flight attendant for TWA. I was driving home on the Garden State Parkway, after a long international flight, and suddenly a poem just appeared in my mind. Out of nowhere! I pulled onto the grassy shoulder of the road and fortunately I had some magazines in the car. I wrote the poem across a page, the whole poem in one fell swoop. It was titled 'Gypsies'. I never wrote another thing for twenty years. 'Gypsies' was published in my first chapbook of poems titled *Blue Edge* from Cervena Barva Press. I still like it.

Do you have a writing routine?

Well, sort of. Every morning soon after waking, before my first cup of tea, I write something. I think my brain cooks up word patterns while I sleep. Many of my poems and stories begin out of a dream that I remember upon waking. Then, throughout the day, lines come into my mind and I write them down. It's an odd thing which is similar to how an actor trains. Actors constantly take classes in-between roles. At least stage actors do this. I was always over at Actors Studio in NYC taking this class or that. It keeps the 'instrument' tuned up. Every Wednesday at the Studio was a 'session', meaning a scene was presented by famous actors. It was a small miracle to be able to watch these sessions and listen to the commentary from the audience afterward. Then every Friday morning the actress Shelley Winters ran a class at the Studio. Free to members. Shelley was such a free spirit and recounted her personal history in between conducting the class. It was mind-boggling! This practice of keep the instrument 'tuned' is pretty much the way my writing mind also works. I feel compelled to write every day. Unless I'm travelling. Then I'm watching and looking and listening and tasting and buying things. The writing comes when I return home.

When you write, do you picture somehow a potential audience or do you just write?

I just write. I never write for an audience, only for myself, only to tell some story that's brewing.

Some writers describe themselves as planners, while others plunge right in to the writing. Would you consider yourself a planner or a plunger?

A plunger. Totally. I'm too independent to be bound to an outline or any set of so-called rules. I never think ahead of a sentence that I just put onto the page. I let the story or poem direct me. I also never use first readers. That practice can botch up a lot of fine work. After all, that's why they make ice cream in thirty plus flavours. Writers have to trust their own instincts.

How important are names to you in your books? Do you choose the names based on liking the way they sound or for the meaning? Do you have any name-choosing resources you recommend?

Character names just come upon me as I write. Lately I've been using the first letter J for my female characters. I think names convey something about a character, and so I let the organic process take over for the naming.

Is there a certain type of scene that's harder for you to write than others? Love? Action? Erotic?

It's all the same. If you, the writer, are immersed, then whatever type of scene you write will be deeply imperative to the plot. I have written some sexy scenes, but not erotica. That makes me slightly uncomfortable. You can have a sex scene without getting into porn. And I only write what is required for plot. I don't arbitrarily throw in a sex scene, or an action scene. Again, I let the characters dictate their plights (plots) to me.

Tell us a bit about your non-literary work experience, please.

When I was in my early teens I made a list of all the jobs I wanted to have. It was long. Some jobs that I had were not on my wish list, but jobs I took out of necessity. Mid-teens I worked in a store called McCrory's in the home goods department. I mainly folded towels that people had messed up. It was a job to get Christmas money to buy gifts for my family. One season working there was enough! I went on to acting school at 16, and worked during the day as a receptionist for GT&E in NYC. It was nice because I was on the top floor where the CEO and those guys had offices. Their secretaries used to let me sneak out and go to acting auditions. It was the perfect job for me at that time. After being a starving actress in NY for a while, I interviewed with TWA to become a flight attendant (stewardess!). They took me but I had to wait 6 months until I was 19 and a half. That was their minimum age requirement. That job changed my life. To travel the world at that young age was simply indescribable. I still have my stew friends and we're in constant contact. I left after 5 years and went back to acting. But I always needed a day job and so I worked for 3 other airlines in Sales and Marketing, and as an Airport Red Coat for United at Newark Airport. When I got married I went to design school and worked as an Interior Designer. I also worked as a singer with bands while I was acting. That was incredible. I've met Springsteen and worked with some of his band. On the dark side, I was a rescue worker in Detroit when Northwest Airlines had that terrible crash in 1987. They sent all their managers out to the crash scene to assist the families of the deceased. That could be a book, unto itself. But I could never write what happened there.

What do you like to read in your free time?
My go-to fiction writers are Graham Greene, Edna O'Brien, Maugham, James Baldwin, and William Trevor. They never disappoint. I also read a lot of contemporary poets. My poet of choice, who was my best friend and mentor these twenty years, is Simon Perchik. Si is deeply missed.

What one book do you wish you had written?
The Power and the Glory by Graham Greene.

Do you see writing short stories as practice for writing novels?
It's hard to say. I think it's different, writer to writer. I began with short stories but quickly wrote a novel that won a big contest.

Do you think writers have a social role to play in society or is their role solely artistic?
To be a good writer you have to be in tune with the world in some way or other. I can't imagine writing in a vacuum. So that brings you into a socially active mode, I suppose. In the worst parts of Covid, I wrote my book *OFFICE* (Wilderness House Press, 2022). But I made it satire, and kind of far-out crazy with plenty of dark humour. I didn't plan on what transpired in that book. Now looking back, I realise I was trying to make some peace of mind for myself. Because I was terribly afraid the pandemic would signal the end of life as we knew it. And it did, until we got the vaccines. The crowded streets of NYC were a ghost town then, with everything in lockdown.

Tell us something about your latest publication, please.
My latest is the novel *OFFICE* which I talked about above. It got a lot of good feedback and a wonderful cover blurb from DeWitt Henry, founding editor of Ploughshares.
I have two more completed novels to come out this year. One quite different from the other. *Hair of a Fallen Angel* takes place in the deep south, and concerns itself with a lot of characters. There is also a surprise plot twist. My protagonist, Janelle (that J again!), lives poorly, and works in a barber shop catering to the mani-pedi aspect of that business. She is also an amazing vocalist and she hooks up with a local guy who made it really big via some nefarious scheme. Of course there's a lot more, but I don't want to give the plot away!
The other book is told in two points of view: The Wife and The Husband. I started that book seven years ago, kept putting it aside for other

projects, and must have done at least 100 revisions. I think it's finally at the place I want it to be.

My big concentration right now is on Playwrighting. I've written five plays and things are beginning to get very interesting in that realm.

Can writing be taught?

That's a hard one. I took a fiction-writing class at The New School, NYC, with an incredibly talented teacher, Alexander Neubauer. Though I'd always been an avid reader, I didn't know the first thing about punctuation, because I never paid attention to it. I just raced through books to get the story. Well, it was this particular teacher (Sandy) who turned on the lights for me. He critiqued everyone's stories, and after my critique he always wrote at the end: 'Keep Writing' with lots of underlines. Wow! I thought, I can do this! We're still friends to this day.

But I also want to add that I don't think writing can be taught. I think craft can be taught. Writing is an art form. I, for instance, could never be a painter. I love paintings, practically grew up in the Met Museum. I might learn the craft of it, but the inspiration to paint just isn't inside me.

Have you given or attended creative writing workshops and if you have, share your experiences a bit, please.

I took a few more writing classes after my class at The New School. From each, I retained something useful. I also studied with author Jamie Cat Callan (Writing From the Right Side of the Brain). Jamie is a very loving and encouraging person. There were eight of us in her private workshop: The Stromboli 8. It was a fabulous experience.

I also taught fiction-writing workshops for ten years. I adored it. My classes were held in a high school, at night, and eventually I taught an advanced workshop that some of those students had requested. It was held in a vintage building, a Quaker Meeting House. There were about seven students and me around a long pine table. Old built-in bookcases surrounding us. It was a beautiful experience that I'll never forget. One of my students went on to win The Mary Higgins Clark Prize twice!!!

Finally, what question do you wish that someone would ask about your writing, and how would you answer it?

Question: Do you live to write?

Answer: Writing has kept me going through thick and thin, so I guess the answer is yes, a resounding yes.

Artist's Statement

Cover image: *Evergreen Ivy*, by Linda Keohane

Linda Keohane works in a few different styles. The leaf work represents the life force in nature. Her other work involves miniature watercolours and large-scale acrylics. She is also a genealogist.

About the image *Evergreen Ivy*

A tiny face painted in oils on a dried ivy leaf sends its quiet message about caring for the natural world.

Biographical Details

Elizabeth Barton's debut poetry pamphlet, *If Grief Were a Bird*, was published by Agenda Editions in 2022. She was a prizewinner in the Shelley Memorial Poetry Competition in 2023. Her poetry has been published in journals such as *Agenda*, *Acumen*, *Mslexia*, *Orbis*, *The High Window* and the podcast *Poetry Worth Hearing*. She is Stanza rep for Mole Valley Poets and leads creative writing workshops.

Sandra Bunting is the author of two poetry collections, *Identified in Trees*, and *Lesser Spotted* and of two collections of short stories, *The Effect of Frost on Southern Vines* and *Everything in this House Breaks*. Her work has been featured widely in anthologies and literary magazines. She is presently working on a novel and seeking a publisher for her children's book, *So Busy*, dealing with climate change and the linesmen who work to keep our electricity on during storms.

David Butler's novel, *City of Dis* (New Island, 2015), was shortlisted for the Kerry Group Irish Novel of the Year. Arlen House brought out his second short story collection, *Fugitive*, in 2021. His literary prizes for the short story include the Maria Edgeworth (twice), Benedict Kiely, Colm Tóibín, ChipLit Fest, ITT/Redline and Fish International awards.

Alicia Byrne Keane's work has been published in *The Moth*, *Banshee*, *The Stinging Fly*, *Acumen* and Dedalus Press's anthology *Romance Options: Love Poems for Today*, among other publications. Her writing has been funded by Dublin City Council, Fingal County Council and the Arts Council of Ireland. Her debut collection *Pretend Cartoon Strength* is published by Broken Sleep Books.

Rachel Coventry's poems appear in *The Guardian*, *The Rialto*, *The North*, *Stand*, *Crannóg*, *Southword* and *The Moth*. Her second collection, *The Detachable Heart*, was published in 2022 by Salmon Poetry. Her monograph *Heidegger and Poetry in the Digital Age: New Aesthetics and Technologies* will be published by Bloomsbury in December 2024.

Enda Coyle-Greene has published three collections: *Snow Negatives* (2007) winner of the Patrick Kavanagh Award in 2006; *Map of the Last* (2013); and *Indigo, Electric, Baby* (2020) all from Dedalus Press. In 2020 she received a Katherine and Patrick Kavanagh Fellowship. She is co-founder and artistic director of Fingal Poetry Festival.

Emily Cullen is the Meskell Poet in Residence at the University of Limerick. Her third collection, *Conditional Perfect* (Doire Press, 2019), was included in *The Irish Times* round-up of 'the best new poetry of 2019'. She is also a harper and a former Director of Cúirt International Festival of Literature. She is currently working on her fourth collection.

Stephen de Búrca is a PhD candidate at the Seamus Heaney Centre in Belfast and received an MFA from the University of Florida. He was selected for the Poetry Ireland Introductions 2023 series. His work has appeared in *Poetry Ireland Review*, *Crannóg*, *Abridged*, *Ninth Letter*, and elsewhere.

Patrick Deeley is a poet, memoirist and children's writer. He has received many awards for his writing. *Cloud Ireland*, his eighth collection, is published by Dedalus Press in 2024.

Laura Demers's short fiction has been published in *Granta.com*, *North American Review*, *The Masters Review*, and *Appalachian Review*. She won the 2021 Denny C. Plattner Award in Fiction and was shortlisted for the London Sunday Times Short Story Audible Prize in 2021.

Patrick Devaney has published four novels for teenagers, including *Rua the Red Grouse* and four novels for adults, including *Through the Gate of Ivory*. His poems have appeared in magazines such as *Revival*, *Boyne Berries*, *Crannóg* and *Skylight 47*.

Anne Donnellan's debut poetry collection *Witness* was published in December 2022 by Revival Press, Limerick. Her work has appeared in several poetry journals including *Skylight 47*, *Drawn to the Light Press*, *Orbis* and *Ropes Literary Journal*. She was the 2023 winner of the Allingham Poetry Competition.

Alexander Etheridge's poems have been featured in *The Potomac Review*, *Scissors and Spackle*, *Ink Sac*, *Cerasus Journal*, *The Cafe Review*, *The Madrigal*, *Abridged Magazine*, *Susurrus Magazine*, *The Journal*, *Roi Faineant Press*, and many others. He was the winner of the Struck Match Poetry Prize in 1999, and a finalist for the Kingdoms in the Wild Poetry Prize in 2022. He is the author of *God Said Fire*, and the forthcoming *Snowfire and Home*.

Attracta Fahy earned her master's in Creative Writing from NUIG in 2017. She won the Trócaire Poetry Ireland Competition in 2021 and the Irish Times' New Irish Writing in 2019. She was placed third in the Allingham Poetry Competition in 2023. She is Pushcart & Best of Web nominee. She has been shortlisted for Saolta Poems for Patience 2023, Fish International Poetry Competition 2022, Write By The Sea Competition 2021, Dedalus Press Mentoring Programme 2021, and Over The Edge 2018 New Writer of the Year. Fly on the Wall Poetry published her debut chapbook collection, *Dinner in the Fields*, in March 2020. She received an Agility Award from the Arts Council in 2022, and is presently working towards a full collection.

Brian Gourley's poems have been published widely in different magazines including *Acumen*, *Northwords Now*, *The Interpreter's House*, *The Honest Ulsterman* & *Poetry Nottingham*.

Kevin Graham's first collection, *The Lookout Post*, was published by Gallery Press in 2023.

Maria Isakova Bennett is a teacher, writer and artist and creates the hand-stitched poetry journal, *Coast to Coast to Coast*. Her awards include The Peggy Poole from The Poetry Society, and a Northern Writers' Award. She has created collaborative work with over 100 poets from the UK, Ireland, and France. She has had five pamphlets of poetry published, the latest, *an o an x* in November 2023 by Hazel Press.

Sai Liuko's poetry has appeared in *3Elements Literary Review, Grimoire Magazine, Honeyguide Literary Magazine*, and others.

Saoirse McCann Callanan has been previously published in *Banshee*.

Denise McSheehy has had two collections of poetry published, the most recent *The Plate Spinner*, with Oversteps Books. Her work has appeared widely in various journals and anthologies. She has received an Arts Council bursary and a grant from the Society of Authors towards work in progress. She is currently working on a collection of short stories.

Mary Melvin Geoghegan has five collections of poetry published, her most recent *As Moon and Mother Collide*, with Salmon Poetry in 2018. Her work has been published widely including *Poetry Ireland Review, Crannóg, The Moth, The Stinging Fly, Cyphers, The Stony Thursday Book, Orbis 184, The Sunday Times, Poems on the DART*, Hodgis Figgis 250th Anthology amongst others. In 2023 she won the Kilmore Quay International Poetry Prize. She is a member of the Writers in Schools Scheme with Poetry Ireland.

Luke Morgan's second collection, *Beast*, was published by Arlen House in 2022 and was described in *The Irish Times* as demonstrating 'a striking, energetic imagination'. His debut collection, *Honest Walls*, was published in 2016. He has new poetry forthcoming from various journals in Ireland and abroad in 2024. As well as a poet, he is also an award-winning filmmaker.

Sara Mullen's poetry and short fiction have featured in *Burning Bush 2, Crannóg, Boyne Berries, The Cabinet of Heed, FLARE, Poethead, Crowstep Journal, Visions International, BlazeVOX, The Journal* and the anthologies *A Thoroughly Good Blue* and *Tearing Stripes Off Zebras*. She holds an M.Phil in Creative Writing from the Oscar Wilde Centre, Trinity College.

Katherine Noone's first poetry collection *Keeping Watch* was published in 2017. Her second collection *Out Here* was published in 2019, both by Lapwing Publications Belfast. Her poetry is published in magazines and journals in Ireland, the U.K. Canada and the U.S.A.

Éamon Ó Caoineachan is a poet and freelance writer. His writing appears in *History Ireland* and *Irish Central*, and his poetry has appeared in several journals, including *The Ekphrastic Review, The Blue Heron Review*, and the *East-West Literary Forum*. He has a master's in Liberal Arts in English and Irish Studies. His first poetry collection, *Dolphin Ghosts*, was published in spring 2021. He is currently writing his PhD thesis on Seamus Heaney at Mary Immaculate College in Limerick.

John O'Donnell's awards include the Irish National Poetry Prize, Hennessy Awards for Poetry and for Fiction, and in 2023 the RTÉ Francis MacManus Short Story Award. He has published five poetry collections, and one short story collection, *Almost The Same Blue*.

Beth O'Halloran is a visual artist and writer. In 2023 her work was shortlisted for the Bridport Short Story Award. She has won and been shortlisted for the Hennessy Award and The Bath Short Story Award. She has been published in both the US and Ireland in publications including the Arlen House anthology *Tearing Stripes Off Zebras*, *Bloom*, *The Ogham Stone* and *Brooklyn Vol. 1*. She is currently revising a memoir.

Jamie O'Halloran won first place in Southword's 2023 Subscriber Competition and was first runner-up in the 2023 Mairtín Crawford Award. Her *Corona Connemara & Half a Crown* was a winner in the 2021 Fool for Poetry Chapbook Competition. Her poems appear in recent issues of *Poetry Ireland Review*, *Banshee*, and *Southword*.

Linda Opyr was the Nassau County Poet Laureate 2011–2013. She is the author of eight collections of poetry and her poems have appeared in numerous anthologies, journals, magazines and newspapers, including *Crannóg*, *Poetry Ireland Review*, *Drawn to the Light Press*, *The Hudson Review*, *The Atlanta Review*, *The Paterson Literary Review*, and *The New York Times*. She was the Visiting Poet in the 1999–2000 Writers Series at Roger Williams University. She has been featured in the 2012 Walking With Whitman Series and the 2002–03 Poetry Series at Long Island University, the C.W. Post Campus; and has served on the poetry faculty of the New England Young Writers' Conference at Bread Loaf. In April 2001 the Suffolk County Legislature presented her with a Proclamation for her work. She holds a Doctor of Arts degree in English and American Literature from St John's University. She was a featured poet in the Bailieborough Poetry Festival in 2017.

Ciarán O'Rourke's second collection, *Phantom Gang*, was longlisted for the Dylan Thomas Prize 2023. His first collection, *The Buried Breath*, was highly commended by the Forward Foundation for Poetry in 2019. Both are published by The Irish Pages Press.

Luke Power's work has previously appeared in various outlets including *New Irish Writing*, *Crannóg*, *ROPES* and *Sonder*. He is working on a collection of short fiction.

Leen Raats is a freelance copywriter. Her poetry and short fiction have been published in *One Art Magazine* and *34 Orchard*. She has won several writing competitions in Belgium and the Netherlands.

Ana Reisens has been published in *Channel*, *Sixfold*, and the Fresher Press Anthology *Winding Roads*, among other places.

Natalie Rice is the author of *Scorch* (2023, Gaspereau Press) and of the chapbook *26 Visions of Light* (2020, Gaspereau Press). Her poems have also appeared in journals such as *The Trumpeter*, *Event Magazine*, *The Dalhousie Review*, *The Malahat Review*, *Contemporary Verse 2*, *Terrain.org* and several others.

Stephen Shields writes both poetry and prose. He has recently been published in *Poetry Ireland Review*, *The Stony Thursday Book*, *The RIALTO* and *Crannóg*.

Beate Sigriddaughter was poet laureate of Silver City, New Mexico from 2017 to 2019. Her poetry and short prose are widely published in literary magazines. Recent book publications include a poetry collection, *Wild Flowers*, and a short story collection, *Dona Nobis Pacem*. In her blog Writing in a Woman's Voice, she publishes other women's voices. www.sigriddaughter.net.

Marc Swan has poems recently published or forthcoming in *Gargoyle*, *Nerve Cowboy Anthology*, *Misfit*, *The Nashwaak Review*, among others. His fifth collection, *all it would take*, was published in 2020 by tall-lighthouse (UK).

Lisa C. Taylor is the author of three poetry collections, most recently *Interrogation of Morning* (Arlen House, 2022) and two short story collections, most recently *Impossibly Small Spaces* (Arlen House, 2018). Her honours include Pushcart nominations in fiction and poetry, the Hugo House New Works Fiction Award, and numerous shortlist designations. Lisa is the co-director of the Mesa Verde Writers Conference in Mancos, Colorado and a fiction editor for Wordpeace, an online journal. Her novel, *The Shape of What Remains,* is due for publication in 2025. www.lisactaylor.com.

Steve Wade is the author of the short story collection *In Fields of Butterfly Flames and other Stories*. His short fiction has won many prizes and has been widely published and anthologised. He has had stories shortlisted for the Francis MacManus Short Story Competition and for the Hennessy Award. His stories have appeared in over sixty print publications.

Mark Ward is the author of *Nightlight* (Salmon Poetry, 2023) and four chapbooks: *Circumference* (FLP, 2018), *Carcass* (7KP, 2020), *HIKE* (Bear Creek, 2022) and the interactive branching sonnet, *Faultlines* (voidspace, 2024). He edits *Impossible Archetype*, an international journal of LGBTQ+ poetry, now in its seventh year.

Stay in touch with
Crannóg
@
www.crannogmagazine.com

Milton Keynes UK
Ingram Content Group UK Ltd.
UKHW050031020524
442040UK00006B/122